"M. L. Stainer's books are wel
own Inglis Fletcher — a group
of the colonial history."

— Harry L. Thompson, Curator,
Port o' Plymouth / Roanoke River Museum

M. L. Stainer, author of *The Lyon Saga* books, has now undertaken an equally serious subject: the story of Joachim Gans, master metallurgist to Elizabeth I, and the first documented Jew in the New World. The story is told from the point of view of Joachim's young apprentice, Reis Courtney, who has volunteered his services to the wild-looking foreigner.

The literary style successfully melds two seemingly incompatible elements: bold action, dramatic choices, blood and gore adventure with its opposite: philosophical meditations on the meaning of life and how to treat others in a hostile world. There is real character development in this 200-page novel as Reis learns the value of a human life. His growing admiration for his shunned master leads him to ponder the various ways of absorbing life's often bitter lessons. Another serious theme concerns the suspicion and prejudice against Jews which the English and Germans brought straight to the New World. The 16th century was one of great superstition—encouraging people in many countries to dread the intrusion of evil entities into the real world. In JOACHIM'S MAGIC a 13 year old boy learns what real magic is and how to become a man in a changing world, where tomorrow is guaranteed to no one. For readers ages 12 and up.

— Gale Finlayson, Historian and College Teacher,
Jacksonville University, Community College of Vermont

To Scott —
Enjoy!
M. L. Stainer

Joachim's Magic

M. L. Stainer
Illustrated by James Melvin

outskirtspress

DENVER, COLORADO

Joachim's Magic
All Rights Reserved.
Copyright © 2015 M. L. Stainer
v3.0 r1.0

Illustrations by James Melvin

Outskirts Press, Inc.
http://www.outskirtspress.com

ISBN: 978-1-4787-5497-8

Outskirts Press and the "OP" logo are trademarks belonging to Outskirts Press, Inc.

PRINTED IN THE UNITED STATES OF AMERICA

To my husband, Frank,
for his love and support

To Lance Culpepper,
whose brilliant portrayal of Joachim fired my imagination

and

To Gary C. Grassl,
whose knowledge of Joachim
helped so much

CONTENTS

PROLOGUE

The Company of Mines Royal, first established in 1568 by Elizabeth I, was created to seek copper and other metal ores in England. Several mines were opened in the Lake District of Cumberland, searching for copper and, hopefully, veins of silver and gold. Recognizing that the English had no real skills in mining, the Queen employed experienced European copper miners, some of them from Germany. By the early 1580's, war with Spain was a serious threat and the sense of urgency was very real to build England's navy in anticipation of future problems. It was of the utmost concern that England replenish her inadequate supply of metal ores without dependence on foreign sources. She needed heavy weapons and good artillery if she were to vanquish Spain. In 1581 at Keswick, a Jewish metallurgist from Prague found himself working under the auspices of the English crown to develop a faster and more economical way to smelt copper. The copper could then be mixed with tin to make bronze, used in canons and other weaponry.

Hearing stories from the New World about the natives

who wore jewelry and decorations fashioned of pure copper, a group of men sponsored by Sir Walter Raleigh and with the Queen's authorization, left England on April 9, 1585 to seek more information about the source of this copper. They hoped to find silver and gold deposits as well. The military leaders were Sir Richard Grenville and Ralph Lane, newly brought back from the fighting in Ireland. After several preliminary explorations, Sir Richard Grenville sailed back to England on August 25 for more supplies, leaving Ralph Lane in charge. Prior to his departure, there had been serious trouble between him and Lane over management of the whole expedition, including an accusation of reckless endangerment made by Lane concerning the raid of the Rojo Bay salt pans. Lane even went so far as to write several letters to his friend and sponsor, Sir Francis Walsingham, Elizabeth's Secretary of State, complaining about Grenville's high-handed treatment.

The head scientist of the group was Thomas Hariot, renowned mathematician and intellectual of his day, and the chief surveyor of the Virginia lands. The vast majority of the 107 members were English and included John White, famed artist and future governor of the Roanoke Colony of 1587. The pilot of their ship, The Tyger, was Simon Fernandes, a Portuguese who later feuded with Governor White on the ill-fated 1587 voyage. When The Tyger ran aground at the inlet of Wococoon, the majority of their supplies and heavy equipment, including a furnace carried all the way from England, were jettisoned to help lighten the load.

Others on the expedition were from the military, called harquebusiers, or musket men. There were also carpenters and those of similar trade skills, some of whom brought their young apprentices with them. In addition, there were a few Irishmen, German miners and the metallurgist from Prague, listed on the records as Dougham Gaunse or Gannes, whose real name was Joachim Gans. He was the first reported Jew in the New World. In his "Briefe and True Report," Thomas Hariot wrote about the expedition, their discoveries and disappointments.

There are those who believe that Hariot knowingly omitted much of the strife and troubles which had occurred.

IN PRAISE OF SEAFARING MEN
IN HOPES OF GOOD FORTUNE

Sir Richard Grenville (The Senior)

Who seeks the way to win renown
Or flies with wings of high desire;
Who seeks to wear the laurel crown,
Or hath the mind that would aspire;
Tell him his native soil eschew,
Tell him go range and seek anew.

To pass the seas some think a toil,
Some think it strange abroad to roam,
Some think it grief to leave their soil,
Their parents, kinsfolk and their home;
Think so who list, I like it not,
I must abroad to try my lot.

CHAPTER 1
REIS COURTNEY

"ME MASTER BEAT me yesterday."

The blond-haired boy moved closer to Reis, his head bent as if tying his bootstrap.

"Now why would he do that?"

The boy cupped a hand over his mouth to hide his words.

"Said I didn't clean his boots well enough."

Reis nodded. He knew Master Snelling, a surly man with a heavy hand which he freely used on his young apprentice. He was always kicking him or raising a fist in his direction. Already he'd yelled at him twice since Hugh stirred out of bed.

"But I HAD cleaned them," Hugh said fervently. "They was a-shining like the sun itself."

He got up quickly, hearing his master's voice bellowing from the camp.

"You'd best be hurrying," Reis warned and watched Hugh run off. Reis sighed, feeling sorry for him. The boy was only nine, after all, torn from his family and still with a lot to learn about keeping on good terms with his master. Many a time since they'd set up camp in this New World, he'd seen him slacking off, leaning against the trunk of a tree with the half-cleaned boots on the ground before him. Now he'd been caught dreaming and whipped for his laziness. Reis wondered how many times he'd be disciplined before he learned. He shrugged. Did no good to worry about another. He was certain the boy would keep incurring the wrath of Master Snelling until he did things right or ran away. Either, at this point, was impossible, for to please Master Snelling would be when the sun fell from the sky and broke into bits and to run away, why, where would he go in this wilderness land of Virginia where home was but a misty dream far across the ocean? Reis gathered his things and walked from the river's edge toward the encampment to find his own master, Dougham Gaunse, thankful he was a fair and just man.

'I be lucky,' he thought, 'for as Master Snelling's apprentice, t'would be hellfire and brimstone for sure.'

Reis could hear the surly man yelling at poor Hugh and he, in return, whimpering and sniveling.

"Crying for your mother?" Master Snelling's voice boomed across the camp.

"Ye be looking for a teat to suck on, Hugh Salter. Never you mind the snot from your nose, pick up them boots and do a thorough job this time. What good be you apprenticed to me? Should I get a stick now and knock your head about?"

Reis watched Hugh walk dejectedly over near the fire, there to keep some warmth in his bones on this cold morn and to get away from his master's wrath. He caught Hugh's eye and gave a sympathetic nod. Wouldn't hurt the boy to know his friend was cheering him on. Hugh nodded back and gave a small smile.

Then he turned and began to finish what his dreaming had made him forget, the careful shining of Master Snelling's boots. Reis saw him spit on the boot to give it shine, knowing in his heart that Hugh was probably wishing it was his master he was spitting on. Reis turned and bumped right into Dougham Gaunse.

"Well," said Master Gaunse with his strange accent, "and what is my apprentice doing, staring at our fire with nothing in his hands?"

He glanced over and saw Hugh vigorously rubbing the boots.

"Aah," he commented, "so it is young Hugh that Snelling was raising his voice to. For what is he being punished?"

"'Twas not what he did but what he didn't do. The boots...," and Reis pointed where Hugh was working close to the fire. Dougham Gaunse nodded.

"A man needs his boots strong and polished in this wild country or the mold will eat the leather and then, they are fit for nothing!"

Reis glanced down at Dougham's boots. They gleamed back at him, the result of his getting up before the sun to shine and spit-clean them so his master would be pleased.

"A good job," said Dougham Gaunse, slowly and thoughtfully pulling on his beard. He nodded his head.

"You are a good apprentice. You serve me well as you learn the trade. *No labor, however humble, is dishonoring.*"

Reis felt a glow in his heart. Praise from Dougham was rare but when it came, it fell like silver rain upon a thirsty land.

"We go digging again, boy. You are game then, to follow and keep the samples?"

"Indeed, sir."

"Then gather the instruments and meet me by the river in five minutes. Forget nothing."

Reis turned and ran back to the tent, there to gather the glass bottles, the measures and weights, the digging implements which were the tools of Dougham's skill in metal, thrusting all carefully into the knapsacks which were strung together. When they were full, he glanced around to make sure he'd forgotten nothing. Then he slipped the harness to which the sacks were attached over his shoulders, buckling the thongs and straps until he felt like a cart horse with his heavy load. He staggered under the weight, righted his shoulders and strode out into the early morning light.

From the distance he saw Hugh watching him enviously. Because of the boots and a long list of grievances on Master Snelling's part, Hugh would be required to remain at camp all day, scrubbing, polishing, sweeping dirt floors, hauling wood from the forest and water from the river. He gave Hugh a cheery goodbye but the youngster merely turned his head away. Reis thought he saw his shoulders heaving.

Then he forgot Hugh in the excitement of another journey. This time they were heading up river about five miles, there to dig the soil and search once again for signs of rock in which might be hidden the iron ores and metals that were Dougham's dream, his life-long vocation. Sir Walter Ralegh had paid Dougham Gaunse's passage across the Western Ocean for just such purpose, to locate copper and other ores for the greater glory of England and her navy. And though Master Hariot, astronomer, mathematician and surveyor was one of the leaders of this expedition, it was clearly Dougham, with his dark eyes and intensity, his thick accent and strange ways, who was favored for his skills as the Queen's own mineral man. The others of the group, some of them Cornwall tin workers and German miners, kept to themselves in the camp and on occasion, had shown discontent at the thought of subservience to such an argumentative and headstrong person as Dougham. Troubles had risen already, but Reis thrust them from his mind as he ran to meet up with his master.

He struggled with his load of sacks which seemed to get heavier with each step. The group of men striding ahead barely glanced back to see how he was faring, nor did he expect them to. They were too busy discussing the possibility of what they might find once they began digging. Already some of the men were arguing, giving vent to loud cries of disagreement. Only Dougham remained calm, walking slowly and pulling always at his black beard. Reis glanced around but there were no other apprentices save for one, a thin, narrow-shouldered boy named Jeremie Whitton, who walked even further behind than Reis, his back stooped under the weight of his master's tools. Jeremie, like Hugh Salter, was about nine or ten. Reis felt so much older at twelve, almost thirteen. He wished there were others his own age, boys he could talk to with some semblance of intelligence. Both Hugh and Jeremie still cried at night for their mothers; he could hear them sometimes when he couldn't sleep for the ache in his own joints.

He often wondered why their mothers had let them go. He had no such concern for he had no mother nor father to care where he was or how he fared. But Jeremie and Hugh had been thrust into apprenticeship back in England by parents too poor to put food on the table. Six silver shillings for the one, seven for the other, a veritable fortune in a shanty landscape so sparse and barren it could barely support its hungry inhabitants. Mothers wept and wrung their hands, fathers cursed and took to their drinks again, but what else was to be done? Masters bound for the New World didn't want females and the girls, bent over sewing or cooking or tending the babes, watched out of the corners of their eyes to see their cousins and brothers sold like cattle to the highest bidder. Hungry eyes the girls had, black as coal dust or else, green like jade only duller, with no light shining in them.

Some of the young boys didn't want to go, kicking and ducking out of the new master's arms which reached for them. Then a swift kick, a curse and a clout on the ear. Back they were dragged, protesting and crying, while the sisters clung to the mothers' skirts, weeping along with them. But silver shillings meant food on the table and the rent paid so they could keep the roof over their heads and not have to sell the last cow. Even the Peter's Pence per annum was too much to give, though out of fear they did so, not wishing to incur the wrath of Holy Mother Church.

Reis was different. Unlike the rest, he had stepped forward and volunteered himself, glad he was older and not so puny-looking. His aunt didn't seem to weep much, he remembered later; his uncle just nodded and gave him a small push.

"See you mind," was all he said.

The aunt, herself surrounded by six or seven youngsters, seemed relieved in a strange, sad way. One less mouth to feed. Reis, who had long ago forgotten how to cry, squared his shoulders and saw his opportunity. He marched right up to the dark-haired, bearded man and said,

"I be Reis Courtney, your new apprentice."

The man laughed a slow, dark laugh, not at all like the Englishmen nearby, but thick with foreign tones. The children stopped weeping, the fathers stopped cursing and they all stared at the stranger who, along with several others, had come into this realm of poverty to seek their helpers.

"Why not in London?" was the question asked. "Why do they come all this way to Surrey when they could have others?"

"Country lads are strong," was the answer, "and all are hungry. Parents will sell their children to keep the landlord from breathing down their necks."

And so for twelve silver shillings, Reis Courtney was apprenticed to Master Dougham Gaunse, to travel with him across the vast, demon-plagued sea to a heathen land called Virginia, named for the Virgin Queen herself sitting on her throne in London Town, in this year of Our Lord, 1585. The aunt took the money from her husband's hand and counted it carefully. It was an immense sum.

The way was getting tangled as they moved further north, keeping the river always to their left. The dig was a greater distance than they'd traveled before and the territory fraught with danger. Savages roamed the thick woods and the men were ever alert. Reis stumbled and would have fallen but caught his balance just in time. His toe throbbed and he realized he'd stubbed it on a stone jutting up from the hard ground.

'Damnation,' he thought then quickly crossed himself. No need to bring the wrath of the Almighty down upon him for his evil tongue! Jeremie Whitton puffed at his side.

"They go too fast," he whined a little, then stopped when he saw Reis's glare.

"Ye need to toughen up, boy," Reis said, sounding just like one of the masters. "This is what we're needed for, to carry the tools of our masters' trade."

"You like it, I know you do. Carrying all those instruments and shovels."

"'Tis not a bad vocation, I must admit. I watch and I learn. One day," he said thoughtfully, "I might be a mineral man just like my master."

"Your master is a strange man with strange ways," Jeremie replied. "I hear the men talking about him all the time. They say he's a heathen, as bad as any Savage."

Jeremie turned his head to glance into the dark woods on the right, as if fully expecting to see a painted figure step from the thickets. He shuddered. Reis smiled. Jeremie was afraid of his own shadow. He listened to every story about the fierce tribes and how they cut Englishmen up into little pieces, skewering them before they were roasted over slow-burning fires. He listened to the stories about Dougham Gaunse, too, from a strange place called Bohemia who was, worst of all, a pagan and a disbeliever in Jesus Christ.

"They say he drinks the blood of Christian babes," Jeremie whispered.

"Not true," Reis snapped back. "Where do you get such ideas?"

"Me master told me and his friend, too. They say Master Gaunse is a Jew."

He spat the word, then quickly made the sign of the cross. Reis said nothing, not wanting the conversation to continue. But Jeremie persisted.

"I've never met a real Jew before. Is it true he killed Christ?'

Reis turned suddenly upon the younger boy, his fists clenched.

"If you mention this bloody nonsense to anyone, I'll thrash you myself!"

CHAPTER 2
THE DIGGINGS

IT WAS BACK-BREAKING work to dig in the partially frozen ground. Already it was November and the snows had come several times, though never lasting long. The men cursed under their breath as they pounded the sullen earth, turning spadeful after spadeful, carefully examining each load for the hidden ores, the glint of metal in the rock. They were looking for the lodestone, the vein which would symbolize their dreams and hopes. Dougham Gaunse joined in with the rest, pushing his feet down hard upon the shovel and heaving it back full of dirt and stones. Every once in a while he stopped to sift through something which perhaps had caught his eye. So intent was he that he never once looked in Reis's direction.

But Reis was a good apprentice to his master, eagerly anticipating his every wish. When Dougham appeared tired, he took his own turn with the digging or else, fetched some refreshment to offer him and the others. None of the men thanked him nor clapped him on the back. Jeremie was equally busy fetching the tools for his master and, since it was only he and Reis, offering his services to the others as well. Reis noted that Jeremie, though young, was more attentive to his master's wishes than Hugh Salter. However, he stayed far away from Dougham and left Reis alone after his threat.

They were searching, Reis had learned early on, for traces of copper and other ore which could be used by the English in their defense against Spain. The Savages wore copper ornaments about their necks, telling the English their sources lay somewhere to the west. Perhaps, Dougham had wisely commented, they wished not to reveal all to the strangers in their midst. Reis had thought Dougham clever for his insight into the minds of the heathen. Maybe it was because Dougham thought the same way, revealing little to his comrades about his origin or his beliefs.

The less that men knew the better, Reis learned from bitter experience, fighting constantly with his younger cousins and their friends who taunted him unmercifully for his lack of parents and wild ways.

For Reis's Uncle Allyn had brought him to his house by coaxing him from the woods where he had hidden for six days and nights after his father's death. A wild boar had gored his father's leg and the loss of blood, coupled with a foul-smelling infection, had been his undoing. As for his mother, Reis had little memory of her save a hazy picture from when he was three years old. She had died, said his father bitterly, of birthing a younger brother who lay alongside her in a grave with no marker. Reis's father had taken to heavy drinking which, no doubt, led to his carelessness in following the boar into its own thicket, where it turned savagely and gored deep his leg. He never did kill the beast but limped back to the hut leaving a bloody trail. There was no man of potions, no one nearby to whom Reis could turn for aid. He ministered to his father as best he could, swabbing the blood and pouring ale on it to try and stem the infection. His father howled as it burned the raw flesh but already it was too late, the wound yellowing and oozing a foul pus of greenish-grey color. A raging fever, complete with delirium, took his father two days hence and Reis, left alone in his anguish, ran off to the woods because he could not bury his father and the stink of his body filled the small hut.

When Allyn came for him almost a week later, he was thin and gaunt with a stomach that howled its emptiness and a fire burning deep in his soul. He ran at first, only approaching when his uncle held bread and water before him. He grabbed the bread and shoved it in his mouth, his large eyes never leaving the figure before him. His uncle was an older man, much greyer in years than Reis's father. He coaxed the boy with bread crusts back to the hut, which they could smell for at least half a mile, it seemed. His uncle cursed and chased the starving dogs away. Then he lit the thatch and burned the hut to the ground.

"A funeral pyre," he grunted. "More than for some, less than for others." He held out his hand and Reis took it, never looking back as the heat of the flames burned away his old life. His gruff uncle brought him to his house and handed him over to his wife. She scowled, then gave him a perfunctory peck on the cheek. It was the last affection he ever received. Reis was seven years old.

By late afternoon the men were exhausted. Containers were filled with samples of rock and earth. The ground became muddied underfoot by the constant march down to the river's edge to fetch water for the sieves. The men rested against the trunks of trees, some dozing, others meditating their own private thoughts. Only Dougham kept working, squatting near the trees while he wrote copious notes in his small neat handwriting. His back was toward the others, for he was as private in his work as in the other aspects of his life. Jeremie and Reis took full advantage of the lull, leaning their aching backs against a convenient pine, glad of the respite. Reis looked at the muddy ground, then at Jeremie. They both knew they would be up early morrow morn to spit and polish the boots again.

"Hey, Dougham," Master Hariot called, "do we go back or make ready for the night?"

Dougham slowly turned around.

"Not much more writing," he answered thoughtfully. "What say you?"

"I say we rest here for the night. I'm in no mind to tramp five miles downstream. We can leave early morn after a good night's sleep."

The others nodded in agreement. One of them called to the boys, "Hey, you, get more wood for the fire. We need to keep it burning all night."

"I knew it," mumbled Jeremie, "always it's us to fetch and carry."

"Best be quiet, boy," cautioned Reis. "This be our job, as I told ye. Come now, no more grumbling."

He and Jeremie got up and walked to the woods' edge, each gathering twigs and branches to feed the fire. Trip after trip they made until they had a high pile of kindling and an equally high pile of sturdy hardwood. They'd had no need of an ax for the wood lay on the ground, dried and ready to burst into flame.

"I've never seen so much wood for the taking," Jeremie said.

"'Tis from the storms," Reis replied. "The wind and rain have knocked these trees about and some lightning too, to make it easier for us." He laughed. "Old Nature must have known we were coming and said, 'I won't work those boys too hard. They be good 'uns, I reckon.'"

Jeremie laughed.

"Indeed we are."

When they had piled enough to satisfy even the sternest taskmaster, Master Hariot sent them down to the river's bank to fetch water for cooking.

"And maybe catch some fish," he added, tossing them a net on a handle.

"Let's see how clever our two apprentices are, what say you, Dougham?"

"Young Reis will catch a thing or two," he replied, hardly turning his head. Reis felt a quick glow.

"Maybe a cold," laughed one of the others. "Certainly not der fisch."

"Let's show them," Reis muttered as he and Jeremie ran to the water. "I know about catching fish, I'll show them all."

"Me, too," said Jeremie, then slid feet first on a patch of slippery mud tumbling straight into the water.

Reis pulled him out, drenched and shivering.

"Best you go back and take off those wet things."

So Jeremie, still sputtering and red-faced, climbed up

the bank and back to the men. Reis could hear their roars of laughter echoing behind him.

"A drowned fish," he heard one chortle. "Never knew a fish could drown itself."

Reis frowned and concentrated on his task. More than ever he wanted to prove himself to the men, but especially to Dougham Gaunse. He'd come back with their supper and wouldn't they all praise him loudly.

He spied an outcropping of boulder over the river's edge and climbed upon it, sprawling himself as far as he could so that the net was extended and he could reach easily into the river's deep waters. He thought he saw a silver fish, then another. He slid the net into the dark water and held his breath. A fish swam near; Reis didn't move. Then another fish and yet another. Perhaps he could catch all three. He moved the net slowly but the fish darted away. Angry, he tried again. It seemed that the fish were teasing him, playing all around the woven net but never going in. Then suddenly luck must have tapped his shoulder, for four fat fish swam right into the mesh and stayed there. Holding his breath, Reis drew the net swiftly out of the water. The silver fish wriggled and flopped but they were caught. Reis gave a whoop of delight.

The supper that night tasted better than anything Reis had ever eaten. The men had praised him as he'd hoped they would. He was made to clean and gut the fish but it was a task he didn't mind at all. One of them produced a pan for frying. Another came from the woodlands with three hares strung from his shoulder, their eyes glazed in death. Reis's stomach growled incessantly for the portions were small, but it was better than going to bed with nothing at all to fill his insides. They even offered him and Jeremie some ale, though Jeremie made a terrible face for the drink was very strong. Reis forced himself to smile as he swilled it down. Only Dougham didn't smile, didn't praise, offered neither approval nor condemnation.

Reis would have felt himself sated beyond belief with praise from his master. It was as if Dougham's earlier words that morn had never been said. Reis fought the surge of disappointment welling in him, filling the vacuum of his stomach and making the fish he had caught so victoriously taste bitter on his palate.

They fed the fire and bedded down for the night, sleeping on leaves they gathered, curled on the cold ground with only a thin cover. Reis listened to the sounds of the night, the snoring of the men, the soft almost imperceptible crying of Jeremie, and thought about his life and lot as apprentice to Dougham Gaunse. It had been a bold and impetuous move on his part to leave his uncle's house and offer himself to a stranger, to a life full of unknown dangers. But talk was rampant about the possibilities in the New World across the sea, of fortunes to be made, lands to be claimed from Spain. 'Twas an opportunity to free himself from the tyranny of poverty which had ground down his Uncle Allyn, his aunt and their seven children. He had made the eighth. Surely that was an impossible task, to wring from the soil enough food for ten hungry mouths. The fire forged in Reis during those days and nights in the woods after his father's untimely death, smoldered within him for almost six years until it flamed high when he saw the bearded stranger standing before him. He stepped forward and proffered his hand, spoke his words and made a pact with himself never to be broken in his lifetime: 'I be Reis Courtney, now your apprentice but always and forever, my own man.'

Enemy Spain was building her territories across the sea in a place called Florida, brazenly sailing up and down the coast. England was years behind in laying claim to those rich and fertile lands. Many, but especially Sir Walter Ralegh, dreamed their dreams of Englishmen in the New World with riches for the taking, building the good Queen's defenses against King Philip. 'Twas Sir Walter who had hired the German miners and one other scientist, Dougham, to traverse the ocean and search the rock and soil of these Virginia lands, eager to find treasures beyond belief: ore for weapons, raw copper to be smelted down and used for England's great fleet, even the hope of silver and gold. To that very purpose, though Martin Frobisher's 1577 and 1578 trips had been deemed failures, there now appeared money in abundance to pay for this new exploration on a ship of great tonnage, The Tyger. Reis had never dreamed there could be so much money in all the world.

The voyage itself had been a rough one, interminably long, full of storms and fury. Two men drowned after being washed overboard by a monstrous wave; another sailor knifed some-one in an argument and was subsequently tied to the corpse to be thrown overboard as punishment, strapped to the very body of the man he murdered. Reis, Jeremie, Hugh and the other apprentices heaved their meager rations at regular in-tervals when The Tyger rose and fell in the waves. Even the masters turned green with sickness and the whole ship stunk with the foul smell of vomit.

"Where is this land we go to?" moaned Jeremie Whitton, clutching his stomach.

"I think it must be in Hell," groaned Hugh Salter and one of the men, his head leaning over a barrel, called out to them,

"You be wrong, boy, 'tis Hell right here!"

Reis spat his bile with the rest of them, ate and vomited again, then willed himself not to give in to the anguish of his stomach. While Hugh and Jeremie moaned and complained constantly, he kept his eyes and ears open listening to the men as they spoke in low voices discussing plans for exploration, what they hoped to find across the sea, what riches might be theirs for the taking.

One late afternoon while they were still upon the sea, its waves quieter than before, Dougham pulled from his pocket a lump of yellowish ore and waved it in front of Reis.

"Why, 'tis gold," Reis gasped, reaching for it. Dougham laughed.

"Fool's gold it is," he replied. "Copper pyrite, made of copper, iron and sulfur. Many are those who think it the real thing. And what of this?"

He produced yet another chunk, this time dark grey. Reis barely glanced at it.

"Foolish boy," said Dougham in his casual manner. "You think this nothing, yet more than three quarters is pure copper. And this," he brought forth still another lump of reddish metal. "Copper comes in many colors, mixed with different ores. Know you your history, boy, and the Romans? They called it *aes Cyprium*, metal of Cyprus. If you be my apprentice, then you must learn these things."

Reis hung his head. He studied the chunks where Dougham had left them, long after his master was snoring away with the others, long after Hugh and Jeremie were whimpering in their sleep. He held them trying to get the feel and touch of them, the weight, the contours, even the smell. Red, yellow, grey, how was he to know which was which? 'Twas a puzzlement and once again, he felt himself unworthy.

CHAPTER 3
DREAMS

THE DREAMS FOLLOWED swift upon each other. The first was of a giant sea monster rising from the depths of the ocean. Its head was larger than two Tygers together, water streaming from its cavernous mouth. Reis stood rooted to the deck, his feet unable to move. The monster swam closer and closer, its eyes black and cold. It lowered its head to devour him. Reis cried out and woke up in a cold sweat. Next to him Jeremie stirred and gave a small grunt. Reis tried to stay awake but sleep took him quickly into another dream.

This time he was hunting a wild boar. The animal was massive, with evil tusks and red eyes. It ran squealing before him then turned suddenly and charged. He dropped his knife and ran, feeling its hot breath upon his heels. The faster he ran the more his feet became mired in quicksand. He found he couldn't move at all. The boar lowered its head to gore him.

In the third dream, Jeremie was drowning in the river and Reis was trying to pull him out. Every time he reached for Jeremie, the boy slipped from his grasp.

"Help me," he called over and over.

"I'm trying," grunted Reis.

"I'm drowning, drowning," called Jeremie and suddenly turned into young Hugh Salter.

"Got to clean these boots," said Hugh, polishing even while the water slid over his face. He disappeared beneath the black waves.

"Too bad," muttered Master Snelling behind him. "I told him to clean the boots well enough."

Reis's heart was beating wildly as he slipped into the final nightmare. He was standing in the corner of a small room. In front of him, Dougham Gaunse was murmuring incantations in a language he didn't understand. Dougham stirred the embers of a fire and from his pocket produced a taper. He thrust the taper into the embers and it caught on fire. Dougham was mumbling and muttering strange, undecipherable words as he read from a book held in his hands. Behind Dougham stood figures, chanting also. One of them took out a knife and slit the throat of a lamb held by two others. The lamb squealed and bleated piteously while its blood dripped to the floor. Dougham took a silver cup and let the blood flow into it, then put the cup to his lips and drank. The dead body of the lamb began to change.

Reis awoke with a start, sweat upon his face. For 'twas not the first time he had dreamed of the lamb, the Lamb of God. Master Lane had named it so when he'd called the men to prayer one Sunday morn in a misting rain. They had gathered together in a somber group, shoulder to shoulder, all except Master Gaunse who stood on the far perimeter near the trees, ever separate and apart. Master Lane had read long and loudly from the Holy Bible. Men were impure, he'd said, condemned forever by the sin of Adam and Eve. God had cast them out of Eden to wander in the wilderness. Only Christ, God's Son, could save them.

"Lamb of God, have mercy upon us," he intoned. In answer to Reis's questioning look the German miner, Master Greutter, had leaned over and whispered,

"Ach, know you the Lamb of God ist Jesus, who vas killed by the Jews."

In his mind Reis saw the gentle white lamb sacrificed, as Christ had been sacrificed upon the cross to save the souls of men. All had bowed their heads and murmured the Holy Words. Out of the corner of his eye, Reis peeked to see Dougham standing, head bent and murmuring also but not the same words. Somehow he knew in his heart that Dougham spoke, not their prayers but his own mysticism.

Around Reis the woods were still; he heard only the low hoot of an owl, the muffled sounds of the men sleeping. He saw Jeremie lying beside him and he was thankful the boy had not drowned in the river's swift current. It had been only a dream, after all. Reis lay on his back staring at the firmament above him with its millions of twinkling lights. He wondered if each light was an angel of God placed there to watch over him. After the dreams, it was a comforting thought.

He heard Dougham's voice coming softly from the trees and half-rose, resting on one elbow to see if he could spot him. But it was too dark and the tree line was in the distance. Reis got up and went away from where he slept to relieve himself against a bush. He heard Dougham's voice again, this time he was sure.

"*Baruch atah adonai eloha-nu melech ha-o-lam.*"

What words were these? Not German, for he'd heard the miners conversing in their gruff, guttural language. His master was kneeling facing the woodlands, his hands clasped in reverent prayer, swaying side to side in a slow rhythm. He wore a fringed shawl draped over his shoulders.

"Master," Reis whispered and the man stopped. He turned.

"Who is there?" he called.

"'Tis I, Reis Courtney. What be you doing?"

Dougham's voice was low and measured.

"I am praying, that is all."

Reis glanced around. "But where be the lamb?"

"What lamb?"

Reis started. This was not a dream.

"Are you real?"

"Indeed," came Dougham's voice. "As real as you, my fine apprentice. What are you doing disturbing my prayers? And what is this lamb of which you speak?"

"Only a dream," Reis murmured, red-faced beyond all measure. "In my dream, there was a lamb sacrificed."

Dougham stared at him. "There is no lamb here," and he swept an arm before him.

"I must go," Reis said hurriedly.

"And what else was in your dream?"

Reis didn't want to tell him how the lamb had turned into the figure of the Christ. He backed away, seeing Dougham's face before his eyes.

The next morn it was as if nothing had happened. Dougham greeted him with a slight nod of the head, not more nor less than before. They were made to fetch water, put out the fire, gather the masters' tools and equipment. When all was ready they began their trek southward toward the main encampment. This time their packs were heavier than ever with all the samples of rock and ore. Dougham carried many of the samples, as did the others. Going back was without breakfast and Reis's stomach growled the whole way. At one point Jeremie left the trail and plucked berries from a nearby bush. He crammed them into his mouth and swallowed them before anyone could stop him. Within a few minutes he began to howl. His eyes teared red with pain and he held his stomach, moaning loudly. Dougham dropped his packs and came running.

"Foolish boy," he admonished, forcing open his mouth. "To eat the yew berry can only mean he has poisoned himself."

"Poison!" Reis gasped. He glanced at Jeremie, beginning to spasm in Dougham's grip. Dougham dropped to the ground, cradling him, then ordered Reis to get a vial from his pocket. Reis handed it to him silently and Dougham opened it and forced the brown liquid contents down Jeremie's mouth. Reis turned away, for Jeremie's eyes were now rolling white in his head and foam was flecking his lips. Thomas Hariot came over but none of the others moved. Dougham forced still more liquid into the boy's mouth and all of a sudden he vomited, spewing out half-chewed berries and bile. Again and again his body heaved until, at length, he lay quiet in Dougham's arms. The man put his ear to Jeremie's chest to listen for his heartbeat, then took a blanket from one of the packs and covered him. He glanced back at the others.

"We stay here for now," he said authoritatively, "until the boy is well again."

Master Hariot nodded.

"So be it."

"What did you give him?" asked one of the men fearfully.

"A tincture," Dougham replied, "to make him vomit."

"Is he dead?" Reis asked.

"No, just resting now. He will be well within the hour. 'Twas not the yew but liken to it."

He got up and left Jeremie wrapped in the blanket. The boy's eyes flickered open and closed several times, then he appeared to be sleeping. Reis scrambled to his feet and ran after Dougham.

"The men are talking," he tugged on Dougham's long cape.

"Why bother me, boy. It matters not what they are saying."

"Witchery," Reis could barely say the word.

Dougham gave a wry smile.

"Not witchery, indeed, merely a potion to release the poison from his body."

"How do you know about such things?" Reis asked boldly.

"I have studied the wild plants and herbs in my native land. Always I keep this nearby," and he patted his pocket, "for the things I have seen men put in their mouths you would not believe. The boy is young and headstrong. No doubt he has learned a valuable lesson."

Jeremie recovered within the hour, as Dougham had predicted. The other men, however, kept to themselves at a distance, talking in low tones while Dougham went down to the river's edge to stare at the deep waters. Reis stayed with Jeremie for a while, then got up and followed his master's trail.

"I saw the men at prayers and kissing their crosses. They are sore afraid. Only Master Hariot said nothing, merely smiling he was."

Dougham frowned.

"Afraid of me?"

"I think so." Reis saw him staring at the cross around his neck. The boy touched it lightly.

"'Twas my mother's, given me by my father. I kept it hidden while I lived with my uncle, for he would have sold it otherwise."

He stared at Dougham.

"Where is yours?"

Dougham looked annoyed.

"I have no cross," he said.

"No cross? Are you not a man of Christ?"

His master frowned again.

"A man of God is what I am," he answered slowly.

"You are not a heathen?"

Dougham shook his head. It was clear to Reis he was getting angry.

"A man of God," he repeated. "Why vex me so?"

Reis turned to go. He heard his master call out behind him.

"Not a heathen but a Jew, one of God's Chosen People."

Suddenly Reis remembered his dream, the incantations, what Master Greutter had said, the blood of the dying lamb, the animal transforming before his eyes. Without a thought to guard his tongue, he blurted out,

"Then it must be true, you killed the Christ?"

CHAPTER 4
THE LESSON

REIS COULDN'T SLEEP after that, his heart sore with wretchedness. How could he have asked Dougham the very question Jeremie had blurted out to him? How could he have been so stupid? Now his master would think him foolish or rash, of no more consequence than a fly buzzing around a dung heap. If he had ever hoped to win Dougham's respect, that hope was dashed by his unguarded tongue.

He tossed and turned the rest of the night, falling into a fitful sleep only toward the dawn. When at last he awoke, the men were up and packing. Jeremie, pale and quiet, was by the river's edge washing the last of the tools. Dougham and Master Hariot were nowhere in sight. Reis gathered his master's possessions once more and strapped them on. He ignored the bread offered by one of the men, a big strapping fellow called Master Haring, kind in his way toward the apprentices.

Hans Haring had been a foreman at the Newlands mine back in England. He was broad-shouldered, with a thatch of dark brown hair. He shook his head when Reis refused the bread, then stuffed it in his own mouth. Though Reis's stomach was once again growling with hunger, the thought of eating made him sick. He was glad Dougham wasn't around at the moment for his face must surely be flushed with shame. He sought out Jeremie by the water and splashed some on his own burning skin. The young apprentice's eyes were huge, framed by his pale complexion.

"I was stupid," he said, lowering his gaze.

"Indeed, you be lucky."

"How close was I then, to dying, I mean?"

Reis smiled.

"Not close at all, just spewing out your innards to the world."

Jeremie clutched his stomach.

"It still hurts."

"A painful lesson," Reis remarked, taking a long drink of water from his cupped palm and thinking, 'I, too, have just learned a similar lesson, perhaps losing the one thing I value most, Dougham's respect.' He shook his head as if to rid himself of such concerns. Jeremie was oblivious to this all, rubbing his stomach and trying to load his master's packs at the same time. He was, Reis observed, quite comical in his actions, much like the monkey he'd seen once dancing at a carnival.

They walked back from the river together and Reis saw, to his dismay, that Dougham had returned and was waiting for him. But his master showed no sign of vexation or discontent. He handed Reis a pick and light auger which the boy took silently, as if the added weight would serve as atonement. The men were waiting in a group separate from him.

"Indeed," Master Greutter's voice came from their midst, "ist Dougham a sainted man or the Devil?"

"Perhaps a physician?"

"Perhaps a...."

"Not one nor the other," Dougham's voice rang out, his accent sounding even more foreign to Reis's ears. "And best you mind your business, Master Greutter. Come, boy," and he gave Reis a push.

"Perchance he is an apothecary, knowing well the medicinal value of herbs."

Reis recognized Master Hariot's calm voice. The others were muttering low.

"That I am," Dougham called back, but his face betrayed the lightness of his answer. His brows were furrowed and his mouth set in a resolute line.

Reis heard some of them still whispering in their German language and not a word of it could he understand. He staggered a little under the weight of his load, then squared his shoulders and caught up with Dougham's long stride.

"Master Dougham," he panted as he came alongside.

Dougham kept walking.

"Master...."

"Hist, boy, bother me not with your prattle."

Reis was downcast as they walked on. He almost had to run to keep up with his master.

"I don't believe you're the Devil," he said at one point.

Master Dougham stopped in his tracks.

"What believe you, then?" he asked. Reis had never heard his voice so cold.

"You must be a healer if you know herbal medicine."

"Heathen?"

"No, Master, healer is what I said. I'm truly sorry for calling you such a word."

Dougham grunted.

"One pang of remorse at a man's heart is of more avail than many stripes applied to him. No matter, for Jews have been called heathens before. Or worse," he added wryly. He stopped and stared at the boy.

"That I am a Jew is of concern to you?"

"Indeed not, for to serve you is an honor...."

His master grunted again.

"It is not a good thing to be a Jew in today's world."

"Why is that?"

Dougham's eyes flashed.

"Look you, boy, for your own self has said the Jews killed Christ!"

Reis hung his head. His very words were coming back to haunt him.

"It's what the others said," he mumbled.

"And you believe what others may say?"

Reis felt like he was choking. For what Dougham said was true. How many times had he listened to the slander of others, or thrown cruel words himself? He couldn't answer and tears suddenly stung his eyelids. What shame had he brought upon himself? What hurtful feelings had he wrought in his master's breast? If he were female, he might have wept bitter tears but instead he wiped his arm savagely across his eyes and stumbled onward as his master led.

Later that night at the encampment, Reis still felt shame marking him. He fetched Dougham's supper and took the mud-caked boots from him. Instead of waiting until the morn, he decided to clean and polish them even if it meant staying up well into the night. He worked feverishly to scrub the leather 'til it gleamed and borrowed wax from Master Hariot, who winked as he handed it to him to work into the surface. When he was finished the boots shone like new. But still he wasn't satisfied. He unpacked the digging implements and scrubbed and polished them, feeling for certain that his arms would drop from his body. It was well nigh the hour of three when he finally completed his tasks. His back ached and his head was dizzy from bending over the tools. He relieved himself at the woods' edge and stretched.

Clouds had covered the heavens and in the distance he heard the faint rumble of thunder. He went back to the fireside and ate the scraps from his supper plate and even those from Dougham's, until he felt the emptiness in his belly fill. But the emptiness in his heart was another matter. For he remembered Uncle Allyn's words to him so long ago: "See that you mind," and he hadn't minded at all but been insolent and outspoken. Surely when they returned to England, his master would request another apprentice. It would be back to the world of poverty for Reis Courtney, of this he was certain. Even if another master took him on, his betrayal of Dougham was a stain forever upon his soul.

He heard his name called and turned to see Dougham beckoning him away from the camp. He laid the plate down and wiped his greasy hands on his pants. Then he followed his master into the woods. For a moment a thought crossed his mind that perhaps Dougham, the Jew, would slit his throat in the dark and somber forest in retribution for his evil tongue. But he pushed the thought from his mind and followed dutifully.

"Sit," was all his master said and he squatted and leaned against the trunk of a tree, waiting to be further chastised.

"Tell me, boy, about the Jews?"

Reis felt his heart begin to pound in his chest.

"I know nothing," he mumbled.

"Indeed?" Dougham's voice was harsh. "Then it be my duty to educate you. Only then will you decide if I am heathen, Savage or, perhaps, the Christ killer."

Dougham began speaking. For well over an hour he told a story and Reis listened. It was unlike anything he'd ever heard before. For in the beginning when God created the Heavens and the earth, He made mankind in His image and called him Adam. He created Eve and their son, Cain, slew his brother, Abel. And years later, when Abraham first heard God's calling, he went to sacrifice his son, Isaac, upon the altar. And God spoke to Abraham and spared his son, and Abraham was the father of all nations.

Dougham's voice had softened somewhat. Reis felt his eyelids drooping as his master neared the end of his story.

"This you have heard before?" Dougham asked.

"My father was not a man of the Bible," Reis answered. He took the silver decoration when Dougham removed it from his neck and placed it in his hand.

"It is the symbol of my people," Dougham said. "Many more stories could I tell you. Perhaps one day…."

Reis studied the intricate design in his hand, with its six points of light. It was different from anything he'd ever seen. He felt its heavy solid weight.

"It is pure silver," Dougham commented. "I keep it hidden so none be tempted. It is called the Magen David, the Star of David."

Then he added decisively."Christ was a Jew."

Reis was startled. He'd never heard anyone say that before. How could Christ, Son of God, the Savior of all mankind, be a Jew, despised by most, feared by many? Dougham must be teasing him. His master saw his face and gave a low chuckle.

"The boy does not believe me?"

Reis hung his head again. Here he was, once more doubting Dougham's word.

"Ask a priest when you return to England."

"I have no priest."

Dougham started to get up.

"Then any of God's clergy. Now it is late, you must get some sleep."

Reis wanted to ask so many more questions. If Christ was truly a Jew, then why did the Jews kill one of their own? Was it true that Jews drank the blood of Christian babes, as Jeremie had said? What was it about the Jews that men hated so much? Why did they speak in that strange language?

"Your prayers, I heard you pray," he blurted out. "'Twas a strange unknown tongue."

For the first time, Dougham laughed.

"That was Hebrew," he said, "the language of all Jewish people. No matter what our place of birth or where we live, all Jews speak the same language. Know you what it means?"

Reis shook his head.

"*Praised art Thou, O God, Ruler of the universe.*" He paused, then gave Reis a push.

"Now to bed, or you will do no work for me on the morrow."

CHAPTER 5
THE BEAR

SOMETHING HAD CHANGED with the men, something imperceptible. Reis noted that they stayed far back from Dougham, though he had always worked alongside them, swinging pick and ax with the best. Only Master Hariot kept up with him stride for stride, on occasion talking earnestly about some new way of smelting, some of Dougham's ideas for a hotter furnace, another ridge of land he wanted to explore.

The Englishmen with the group strode forward, talked a while then fell back. Only the German miners kept their distance, gesturing and muttering in their guttural tones. At one point, Reis saw Master Hariot clap Dougham on the back.

"Pay no heed," Reis heard him say but though he strained his ears, Dougham's reply was lost in the soughing of the wind through the branches. The storm, which had held off from last evening, was fast approaching. The thunder boomed and lightning lit the treetops.

"We'll be caught in this," Thomas Hariot called and signaled the men to hasten. But just as he spoke the rain came whipping down, drenching them all. It was a cold rain full of the promise of snow. Reis could hear the men cursing, English curses and German ones. He didn't blame them. The rain made the going difficult; the wind blew with fierce intensity. He was bitterly cold and thoroughly soaked by the time they reached the last mile.

"The last is the hardest, eh lad?" Master Hariot gave him a smile. He looked as comical as the rest, with his hair slicked down and his hat's brim filled with water which dripped, also, from his beard. Reis blinked his eyes to clear them. Behind him, puffing and panting, Jeremie slogged through the rain and mud.

"My stomach still hurts," he complained.

"And probably will 'til you shit the rest out. What a blockhead you were," and Reis laughed. Then he suddenly remembered Dougham's words and was instantly sorry. Jeremie sniffled and wiped his arm across his nose.

The sky lit up with lightning and they watched as a bolt ripped the heavens in two and streaked down toward the woodlands. There was a thunderous crack and the smell of sulfur in the air.

"A tree's been struck," called Master Hariot and at almost the same time, a fearful bellowing arose. The men stopped in their tracks. Master Hariot reached quickly for his musket and powder.

"Damnation!" he exclaimed. "The powder's wet."

"Not mine," said Master Haring, stepping forward. "See." And he pulled a pouch of powder from under his thick cape.

"I keep it close to mein heart," he laughed heartily, then repeated it in German for the others. They, too, began to laugh.

Thomas Hariot took shelter under Master Haring's broad cape and quickly loaded the musket. He cocked it and held it at the ready.

"A wick," he called. "Quickly now."

Jeremie tugged on Reis's arm.

"What is it? What is making that horrible noise?"

"Why, 'tis a bear," called Master Haring in his thick voice. "A great big bear, mean and angry. Hungry for the likes of a young boy."

Jeremie gasped.

"Don't tease the lad," Master Hariot said, stepping out to face the woods. Just as he did, a large brown animal came lumbering directly toward them.

Jeremie squealed loudly, the men cursed. Some of them held their ground, others ran toward the river's edge. The bear saw them and stopped abruptly, rising up on its hind legs. It gave a mighty roar. Master Hariot struck the flint and held it to the wick, which quickly caught. The wick flared against the powder and the ball flew speedily with a loud cracking sound. Master Hariot's shoulder took the force of the musket's kick but the ball hit the bear squarely in the chest. The anguished animal screamed its rage and pain, dropped to all fours and took a few more lumbering steps. Then it fell to its side. It tried to raise its head but quickly expired. The men gathered around Master Hariot, those who'd headed toward the river came running back. Jeremie was jumping up and down.

"Oh, you hit it, you hit it!"

"Hist boy, stay clear. It may still have some life left in it."

Without hesitation, Master Haring took his knife and moved swiftly to the fallen beast. He kicked it once then grabbed its head and slit its throat. Reis saw the thick, dark blood rush out to be washed away in the soaking rain. He watched Master Haring hack off the head and hold it aloft.

"The prize ist yours," he said victoriously. Then he walked over and presented the head to Thomas Hariot who took it, bowing in acknowledgment.

"What was that all about?" Jeremie whispered to Reis.

"The head of the beast," Reis answered, "goes to the one who made the kill."

By now the rain was lessening and the men decided not to trek the last mile but to rest and take what they wanted of the meat. Under a sheltering rock, they managed to build a fire, sputtering though it was, and Masters Haring and Greutter carved sections of the bear and wrapped them in cloth to bring back with them.

They roasted a portion of the leg over the fire and while it cooked, laughed and joked and drank some ale. It was the first time Reis had seen them relax since The Tyger laid anchor.

The smell of bear roasting made Reis salivate. When Master Haring handed him a chunk of sizzling meat, its juices running out, he burned his mouth in his haste to stuff it in and promptly spat it out. Master Haring laughed, then simply speared him a second piece. They ate ravenously for the dried meat, bread and vegetables which they'd been eating tasted nothing like this succulent meal. Reis watched Dougham shake his head at the proffered meat, then pull out some bread and eat that instead. Again he shook his head and waved the portion away when Master Haring pressed him. From the group Erhart Greutter's voice called out,

"Our famed Dougham does not eat bear meat?"

Dougham didn't answer but got up and went to the edge of the clearing. The rain had lessened; only a tell-tale echo of thunder was heard in the distance. Even the trees ceased rustling.

"Essen, essen, Master Gaunse," Greutter's voice came again, a mocking tone to it.

"Or are you perhaps too gut mit uns essen?"

"Silence, Erhart," said Thomas Hariot with authority. "A man may choose to eat what and where he wishes and leave what he does not want."

Jeremie poked Reis hard in the ribs, his mouth full.

"I told you, didn't I, his religion forbids him to eat meat."

"That's not true," Reis replied. "For I saw him eat...," and then he stopped.

Perhaps it was true, after all. When the man had brought the hares back to their diggings, his master had refused those as well, preferring to eat the stale bread and thick cheese. Why would Dougham not eat of this delicious meat? He got up and fetched some ale to bring to him. "Master," he said and offered the mug. Dougham took it.

"The meat is delicious."

"Eat then."

"I can get you a choice piece."

"I cannot eat of it."

"But why...?"

Dougham said nothing, so Reis persisted.

"But why not?"

"Because it is unclean!" Dougham snapped suddenly, turning around to face him. His eyes were flashing. "It is not sanctified...."

He stopped and turned away again.

"No fault of yours," he began, "but this is not your concern, only mine.... Go back to the others, young Reis, and eat your fill, Trouble me no more."

He stood there not saying another word. Reis shrugged his shoulders then and went back close to the fire. He shoved the chunk into his own mouth so they wouldn't notice that Dougham hadn't taken it. What a strange man his master was. Perhaps Master Greutter was right, and the others as well. To turn down meat when one was hungry.... It just didn't make sense!

The men divided the bear evenly, which only added to their loads and the packs that Jeremie and Reis carried. Master Hariot ordered them to dig a large hole and bury the carcass, "to keep the wolves from coming," he said. Under great protest the men dug a pit and covered the remains with earth and rocks. It was late when they returned to the encampment, greeted with loud cheers by those who stayed behind.

But Jeremie's and Reis's jobs were not over. They had to unpack the bags and those of their masters, then take the bear meat to the smoke house where Master Bremige hung the pieces on large hooks over a smoky fire.

"First ve smoke it," he said in his thick German accent, "then ve hang it und store it. This way ve alvays haf food. Ist gut?"

Reis collapsed at the end of the day, near exhaustion. His shoulder muscles were sore and his back ached. Hugh Salter came running over. "You were attacked by a bear?" he asked, his mouth agape. "How big was it, how fierce, did it kill anyone?"

"It was of good size," Reis said and, seeing the boy's excited face, added, "indeed, 'twas a fearsome creature and when it stood on its two hind legs...."

"Master Hariot shot it readily," Jeremie embellished the story, "but yet the bear moved and twitched its legs. It made to stand...."

Reis laughed and held up his hand.

"Enough," he said. "Master Hariot finished it right off. But still it was a terrible fright."

Hugh made them tell the story over and over again, how the lightning split the sky asunder, how the giant oak tree fell and scared the bear out into the open, how Thomas Hariot's aim was steady and true, how the bear fell with the ball deep in its chest.

"And what of you while we were gone?"

Hugh shrugged. "I cleaned more boots than I can count and I scrubbed Master Snelling's tools and cleaned the huts and...."

"Hold! You worked as hard as we did."

"I wish I'd been there," Hugh's voice was full of envy. "I wouldn't have been scared. I wouldn't have run away."

"No time for either," Reis smiled. "But you stayed drier than we did."

After a while Reis got up to clean and polish Dougham's muddied boots, and help Master Hariot clean his weapon. Dougham was once again nowhere in sight, so he readily went to fetch the musket for Master Hariot and watched him take it apart to clean the barrel.

"Always keep your weapon clean and at the ready," he told Reis. "For, like the bear today, you never know when you might need it."

"I wish I could shoot like that."

"Indeed, has no one shown you?"

Reis shook his head. In truth, he had never seen Dougham shoulder a musket.

"Then I shall teach you," Master Hariot smiled. "For 'tis a good thing to know how to protect yourself."

CHAPTER 6
QUESTIONS

"MASTER HARIOT...," REIS began, but hesitated. He wanted to ask him about Dougham Gaunse, to learn more about his master. But he couldn't find the right words.

"I see you're puzzled."

"I have many questions and no answers."

"Questions about...?"

Reis hesitated. How could he ask without violating Dougham's trust? But Master Thomas Hariot seemed to sense what it was he wanted to ask.

"Your master is a man of few words."

Reis nodded. For certain, the most Dougham had spoken was when he told him the story of Abraham.

"But each word carries its weight. Do you understand what I mean?"

Reis thought for a minute.

"Yes," he said. "For I know what he wishes without many sentences strung together."

"Is he a good master?"

Again Reis thought.

"He doesn't beat me."

Thomas Hariot laughed out loud.

"Indeed, then that makes him a good master, I'll wager. No boy likes a whipping. So what puzzles you?"

"He didn't eat the bear meat when I offered him some. Nor the hare before. Why is that?"

"Aah." Master Hariot leaned back, placing the cleaned musket by his side. "You think that strange then, that a man doesn't eat meat?"

"He eats no meat," Reis suddenly remembered. "Only bread and cheese and whatever vegetables we have. And then he says prayers over it."

"He speaks in Hebrew, you mean?"

"That's the language he uses. At first I thought it was a form of German but it's different."

Master Hariot eyed him with a clear look.

"Master Gaunse is a Jew. Did you know that, boy? His religion prevents him from eating certain foods. He can only eat the flesh of an animal that has had special prayers said over it. A rabbi could bless his meat but there is none here. He can eat no swine, either."

"What's a rabbi?"

"A holy man, like a priest."

Reis suddenly understood. Dougham couldn't eat the bear meat because it hadn't been properly blessed.

"Why could he not have said his own prayers over it?"

Thomas Hariot smiled again.

"It is not the same, according to Dougham." He reached over and clapped Reis on the shoulder. "It's quite compli-cated, isn't it, a man and his beliefs? We must each respect the other. Dougham Gaunse is a serious student of the Talmud."

"What's that?"

"Jewish tradition and spiritual wisdom. He studies the ancient books, as do many of our scholars. The study of Hebrew is quite fashionable throughout Europe. As learned men seek answers to Biblical questions, they turn to the original source. Master Gaunse is always quoting from the Talmud, have you not noticed, boy?"

Reis remembered then some of the sayings Dougham had muttered from time to time. *"Few are they who see their own faults,"* when Reis was annoyed at being chastised: *"The ass complains of the cold even in July,"* when he overheard Jeremie complaining of his load: *"Silence is the fence around wisdom,"* when Reis kept asking questions.

"Since he healed Jeremie, the men are sore afraid of him," Reis ventured boldly, then bit his lip. He was telling the man too much.

"They are afraid out of ignorance. As you see, boy, I am not afraid of Dougham Gaunse, neither is Sir Walter Ralegh, who hired him. He is a skilled man and his ideas will change the way copper is smelted and used. For this, I brought him with me to the New World. For this, Sir Walter Ralegh and our good Queen Elizabeth have paid his way. Know you that we near war with Spain?"

Reis nodded.

"Last year the Spanish envoy was expelled from London. Ever since they seized our ships in Iberia, we have been preparing for war. Now there is open hostility between our two countries which will wreck the plans for our venture if we allow it. Copper and tin ore are sorely needed for our navy. For this reason, Sir Richard Grenville has sailed back to England, leaving Ralph Lane as our leader, to tell the Queen of our findings here in Virginia. For this reason, Walsingham commissioned the services of Dougham Gaunse.... Jew, Gentile, it matters not. It is his skills we seek and for those, we shall offer him our dutiful respect."

Reis went back to his place near the fire feeling a bit more comforted from Master Hariot's words. It was obvious that Dougham was a man of great importance, favored by both the Queen herself and Sir Walter Ralegh, favored by Thomas Hariot as well. He was fortunate to be apprenticed to such a man. Dougham's peculiarities paled beside his new-found understanding of his master's work. He was a skilled mineral man, Master Hariot's exact words, and Reis could learn a great deal from just watching him.

He thought about his master's dark flashing eyes, his black unkempt hair and beard, his incantations and ways of praying which were strange to him.

"It matters not," he mumbled to himself, "for he is a great man. It must be so, for Master Hariot has surely spoken truth."

He dreamed again of a heavily bearded man wielding a stick which flashed fire and brimstone. This man was not the Devil for he had no horns growing from his head. But he was dressed in black like the Devil, and wherever his stick touched the ground, flames sprang from it.

"Stay away," said this man in a foreign-sounding voice. "For if you challenge me, I will slay you."

Reis ran to hide behind a tree but the man's stick found him out and set the tree afire with a tremendous blaze. He ran to another tree but the same thing happened. The forest was burning all around him and he heard the man laughing in a deep voice,

"You can not escape the power of the Jews. Try as you may, we will find you out."

He awoke with a start, sweat covering his brow and his body. He got up and stumbled to a bush to relieve himself. The cold night air set a chill about his body and he began to shiver. Looking behind him he saw Master Hariot still sitting by the fire, reading and making notes much the way Dougham did. He walked back to the warmth of the fire and up to Thomas Hariot again.

"Young Reis, you're still up?"

"I had a nightmare," he said, feeling relieved to share with someone and embarrassed at the same time.

"Was it a monster?"

"Someone who looked like the Devil and set trees on fire."

"Oh, a really bad dream."

Master Hariot didn't laugh or even smile.

"I have another question," Reis said then.

"Perhaps you have too many questions on your mind and they are causing these dreams."

"Perhaps," he shrugged.

"Ask me your question, then."

"Did the Jews kill Christ?"

Thomas Hariot stared at him for a long time.

"That is a question that scholars have pondered for a long time. I'm not sure there is a definite answer to it."

Reis stood there and the man continued.

"Christ was a Jew and a rabbi. He preached about the

Kingdom of God. Many of the Jewish officials and religious men didn't like what He was preaching. So they turned on Him and surrendered Him to the Romans."

"So they DID kill Him!"

"Not by themselves. They used the Romans to get rid of Him."

"Was He the Messiah?"

"The Jews don't believe He was. The Christians do. That is the difference between them."

"But He was a great man?"

"Yes, indeed, whether rabbi or Messiah, He was indeed a very great man."

Reis yawned and rubbed his eyes. All this information was fogging his brain.

"Time for bed," said Master Hariot and turned back to his writings.

Reis fell asleep right away and no more dreams plagued him that night. In the morning they were called for more work.

CHAPTER 7
THE COPPER FURNACE

A PORTION OF the crude assay furnace and its shelter had to be rebuilt. During the storm a tree had fallen nearby and one large branch had smashed the far supports and corner of the brickwork. Master Greutter and Hans Altschmer talked loudly in German as they cleared away the twigs and leaves, removing the crumbled brick. A third man was called over and the trio worked to set new support beams and repair the roof. The furnace was patched and repaired as best they could. Master Dougham came to inspect along with Thomas Hariot and Randall Mayne, one of the smelters.

"A fair job," commented their leader and Master Mayne nodded in agreement. Dougham Gaunse just grunted.

"What's the matter, Dougham?" Hariot asked.

"The hearth slants," he said finally. "I am not pleased. In this makeshift furnace the liquid ores will pool in one corner unless fixed."

Hariot squatted down to look.

"You're right," he agreed. "It must be torn down and rebuilt."

He called to the others.

"The furnace must be taken down and completely rebuilt."

"Nein, und?" asked Master Altschmer.

"It slants downward. The angle is incorrect."

"Verdammter Jude!" muttered Master Greutter angrily.

He joined Altschmer by the furnace. Hariot showed them the problem and they threw up their hands, spouting in German. "Dougham will supervise," concluded Master Hariot as the two men stared.

"Master Gaunse is in charge of the furnace," Hariot repeated authoritatively.

The two went to tear down the structure, giving Dougham and Hariot angry looks.

Reis, Hugh and Jeremie were called upon to help. They took the bricks which were removed and cleaned the area. Then they mixed the mortar for the new brick and filled the trowels.

"Verdammter Jude," repeated Master Greutter, then caught Reis staring at him.

"Was wollen Sie?"

Reis couldn't understand the German words but thought it was a curse against his master. He kept as impassive as possible when Master Greutter was looking but made faces at the back of his head.

Hugh and Jeremie tried not to giggle.

"Vat ist so funny, boy?" asked Altschmer.

"Nothing, sir."

"You laugh at us?"

"No sir, no indeed."

Reis was glad when the work was finished. The furnace

floor looked level to him. Master Hariot came to inspect, took measures and checked the angles. He nodded to Dougham.

"Good," he said.

"Hmmm...," was all Dougham said.

Master Gaunse called it a makeshift substitute, for his great metal furnace brought all the way from England had been thrown overboard along with other equipment when The Tyger foundered at the inlet of Wococoon. Though he had protested mightily, Tyger's load had to be lightened. To that event, Dougham refused to speak again with Simon Fernandes who had caused the problem, as Dougham angrily stated, "by his poor navigational skills."

The furnace was used for smelting the raw ore. There were actually two hearths. One, as Master Hariot had explained, was for the casting of copper, the other for heating it for the hammering. Each of the hearths had a great pair of double bellows with iron chains for fanning the flames to a high temperature.

Each forge was supported with huge bows of iron. There were two pairs of strong iron shears which were used to cut the copper, several tongs, some hand hacks, a hatchet, two great hammers and two punch irons to hew the metal. There were anvils, ladles, wooden trays and a large barrel kept full of water at all times. Glass bowls were everywhere. Weights and measures used in determining the value of the ores were on nearby shelves. The shelves where the furnace was housed was much like an alchemist's workplace, a small factory for producing and refining raw materials. Reis was especially fascinated by the long instrument which was in the shape of a hollow tube, anchored over the flames on a fulcrum and angling down to a glass ball where the liquid pooled to be drawn off. It was there, Master Hariot explained, that the raw ore was first tested "for its properties."

Reis noted that the men who worked the fire to roasting were always red-faced and blistered from bending over its heat, sweat glistening their foreheads and often running down their cheeks into their beards. If the fire burned falsely, there was biting smoke which caused the lungs to ache. Sparks flew whenever the bellows belched air to fan the flames, jumping off the coals onto hands and bare arms. 'Twas not a job for the weak, untrained or feeble-hearted, for much skill was needed to know how hot to let the fire burn, how long to keep the crude ore cooking, how to judge when the liquid was ready to be skimmed off.

There were many other alchemist tools around, crucibles for holding molten ore, ointment pots, scraping knives, iron trivets, files and pincers, measuring angles and things which he knew not, neither their names nor uses. Master Gaunse had promised to teach him the skill of a mineral man but there was so much to learn.

On the long and endless trip from England when the storms roared and no man dared go topside unless he was a sailor and even then, his life was forfeit, Dougham sat with him and told him of the mysteries of copper and its properties. Of his own ideas, his master was more secretive, sharing none of his thoughts on what he hoped to accomplish. But Reis learned a great deal about copper.

"Antimony," said his master, holding up an odd piece of metal, "antimony sulfide. For use as a flux to separate silver from the metal." And when Reis stared at him he added, "silver is… drawn to the sulfur it contains. Not only do we seek copper to make bronze but silver as well, perhaps even gold."

'Ah, gold,' thought Reis, 'gleaming yellow gold. Gold to fill one's pockets and buy all things, gold to dance around, gold of the sun, gold….'

"Be you day-dreaming, boy?"

Reis shook his head.

"How is bronze made?" he asked then, snapping himself back from his dreams..

"By mixing copper with tin. And bronze makes the English cannons strong against the Spaniards," added Thomas Hariot with a laugh. "Bronze does not corrode in the salt air. Did you know that, young Reis?"

"No sir."

Dougham grunted.

"My apprentice is full of ignorance. *You can educate a fool, but you cannot make him think.*"

"Here now, Dougham, the boy is no fool. He is quick to learn." Master Hariot winked at Reis.

Reis was glad Thomas Hariot, the great mathematical genius, appeared to favor him. It made his efforts to please Dougham somewhat easier. For Dougham Gaunse was a hard taskmaster, not in the same way as Master Snelling with his quick tongue and ready strap, but in another way. Dougham had such high expectations, it was well nigh impossible to please him and praise was not swift in coming.

As he listened to the men while on the sea, Reis learned just how much of the harsh German language was incorporated into the mining of copper.

Master Mayne had said, "Ach, ve hope to find the stein to be fett. If ist durr, then for nothing ist our vork."

"What do those words mean?" Reis asked curiously, for Master Mayne seemed friendly enough.

"Stein comes from our first smelting. Ist iron und copper sulfides together. If it ist fett, ist rich in silver. If durr, then barren of silver. Go now," and Master Mayne gave Reis an amiable push. "Go tell your master how you sprechen Deutsch."

Reis hoped to impress Dougham with this new-found knowledge but Dougham, in his usual manner, just grunted. Reis was sorely disappointed. He busied himself checking the ropes which held the barrels and crates for all the instruments to be used when the vessel anchored in the Virginia lands. The sea tossed them like corks in a bottle, first one way then another. They were all sick and vomited their food. 'Twas a fearsome rough crossing, Master Lane had said, as if the mighty ocean was firm in its mind to drown them all. The Tyger groaned and creaked and shuddered in the force of the waves, but it proved seaworthy enough and they reached the far shores only a little off schedule. As the men built their encampment and the shelter to house the furnace, Reis marveled at all the equipment they'd managed to bring with them. The holds of The Tyger must have been jammed full of it, for the darker depths of the ship he'd not been privy to. Quite possibly a great deal of this equipment was stowed aboard the other ships that had sailed with them, The Red Lyon of Chichester and the three flyboats, Dorothy, Roebuck and Elizabeth. Each ship housed many men: harquebusiers, swordsmen and long bowmen for their protection, and the tradesmen needed to construct the encampment: carpenters, grubbers and rooters up of trees, coopers to make barrels and all such manner of skilled men. On board The Tyger with them was Master Hariot, famed astronomer and mathematician, a physician, an alchemist and a man who studied gemstones called a lapidary. John White, the artist traveled with them and Simon Fernandes, who had flooded their supplies by carelessly running The Tyger aground at the inlet of Wococoon, angering Dougham over the loss of his mighty furnace. Fernandes, Reis overheard Hariot tell Master Lane, was a troublesome man.

One late afternoon as they watched the men stoking the fires of the furnace yet again Dougham, in a generous mood, told Jeremie, Hugh and Reis himself of the wondrous nature of copper.

"Copper ore that shines is sulfurous. Blue, green or brown ore makes much copper but the yellow shining is what we want, for that gives up a finer and more silvery result. And not too high a flame, careful, or the metal will breathe out the sulfur and then we will have only a burnt slag. Keep your calcining fire low and burn the ore until all blue flame be gone."

Hugh had become bored with Dougham's talk and Master Snelling's calling had come, surprisingly enough, as a welcome break. Dougham stared after him and murmured,

"He who adds not to his learning diminishes it."

But Jeremie and Reis continued to sit and listen as the master explained the complicated smelting process.

"We take the ore out and cool it in cold water, then stamp it into pieces as small as hazel nuts. Know you, boy, it sweats under a slow fire for twenty-four hours until the taste and smell of sulfur is gone. Then raise the fire high and get the ore to liquid again and be quick about it so the slag will not mix or feed on the metal. We separate it upon cooling and stamp it again, and for a third time stoke in the furnace until it flows smooth. Skim the green regulus and coarse copper is what we have."

By now Jeremie was yawning so Dougham excused him.

"And what of you, my fine apprentice, do you wish to hear more or are you asleep in your britches?"

"More, sir."

Dougham seemed pleased."The dross separates by our purging and refining. If what is left is not malleable, into cold water it goes."

"And how do you find the silver?"

"Aah, if silver hides there we will find it by adding antimony and even lead. Know you that silver will sink down to the lead? And all this," Dougham nodded thoughtfully, "is what Agricola described in his book, De Re Metallica."

From deep in his pocket he produced a volume of notes, all in his fine painstaking script. He gave a deep sigh.

"Perhaps one day I, too, will produce such a work."

Reis never realized there was a whole science of metals and their properties, that men had actually written books about it and spent their entire lives devoted to this study of ore. He bade Master Dougham a good night and went to bed, tired but unable to sleep. Tossing and turning fitfully, he finally fell asleep dreaming of cauldrons filled with liquid copper bubbling and frothing. But instead of mineral men gathered around, black witches chanted as they stirred the effulgent mixture.

CHAPTER 8
AN ALARMING DISCOVERY

REIS KNEW LITTLE of politics; the only kind he'd come in contact with was when the local tax collector came for his revenue. Then he'd heard plenty from Uncle Allyn and the others, how they paid too much and could scarce make a living, and what was their good Queen doing with poor people's money except to build her navy?

But the fact that England was building ships and huge cannons in anticipation of future war with Spain intrigued him. He thought that King Philip of Spain was a bad ruler for trying to take advantage of the English Queen. After Henry VIII died, Elizabeth's half-sister, Mary Tudor, had become Queen. Catholic Philip had married her and so, Mary had turned the country once more to Catholicism. Then Mary died and when Elizabeth took the throne, Philip had actively pursued the young queen. If Elizabeth married him, then England would return to its "papal ways," as Uncle Allyn said. It had been very bad for the Anglicans under Bloody Mary's rule but with Protestant Elizabeth as Queen, the persecutions had stopped and it was the Catholics who worried now.

"And those who plot against her," said Uncle Allyn, nodding his head. "'Tis treason to rebel against our Queen."

Reis had heard tales of the terrible things done to traitors, floggings, torture, heads chopped off. It was not a good thing to anger this fiery queen with her flaming red hair. Luckily, she looked with favor upon the brave men who went off to explore the New World and bring back treasures for her coffers. Much money was needed if England planned to win against Spain or any other country who challenged her supremacy. I am, Reis often thought, more than the lowly apprentice of Dougham Gaunse; I am a brave explorer in this wild land across the sea. His chest puffed with pride and he strutted around like a cockerel until he saw Dougham watching with with his dark, intense eyes.

"Ah, boy, *know you that the sun will set without thy assistance.* Be you gone."

Then all his pride collapsed as if pricked with a pin. Dougham had taken him for a fool!

One of the men fell stricken with the ague, then another and yet a third. Reis found himself working the furnace alongside the smelter called Hans Altschmer. It was backbreaking, blistering work. Reis's job was to work the mighty bellows, opening and closing them so the air fanned the flames to an intense heat. He sweated constantly, feeling the trickle down his back and on his face at all times. Only when the fire was of sufficient temperature was he allowed to put down the bellows. But his work wasn't over. He heaped the green ore in piles before its preliminary roasting and shoveled the left-over slag into buckets for carrying away and dumping. He arms felt like they were being torn from their sockets and he noticed one day, to his intense dismay, that blisters had formed on his bare skin from the fire sparks which danced and whirled in the air.

Master Altschmer noticed his arms when Reis was examining them.

"You hast the marks of a true smelter," he roared with laughter. Reis couldn't help smiling.

"I'd rather not be a true smelter," he replied.

"Honest marks," nodded the man. "comes mit gut hard vork."

Reis liked Master Altschmer but only when he was working by himself. When he was with Master Greutter he became just like him, muttering all the time in his guttural German tongue, sneering when Dougham came near. When Dougham came to examine the liquefied ore, to take his samples and test them again and again, Master Altschmer kept silently working the fire, saying not a word one way or the other. One time Reis felt a boldness come upon him unlike anything he'd ever experienced before.

"Why don't you like my master?"

Hans Altschmer stopped feeding the fire and stood straight up until he towered over Reis.

"Vat ist this vat says I do not like him?"

Reis began to tremble. He didn't want to anger this man with the powerful arms which could easily crush him like an insect.

"You say?" asked Master Altschmer.

Reis could only nod.

"Hmmm," said Altschmer, stepping back from the flames. He paused for a few moments before he spoke.

"He ist Jude...."

"And I'm English and an Anglican," Reis blurted out. "So...?"

For a moment Hans Altschmer turned as red as his fire. Then without warning, he threw back his head and roared with laughter. Reis stepped back, for his laughter made the very timbers of the furnace room shake.

"You are brave boy, as vell as English."

"Why don't you like the Jews? Master Dougham is a great scientist."

"His science ist not vat bothers me."

"But you judge him on his beliefs?"

Master Altschmer thought for another moment.

"He ist Jude... a Jew, as you say. Enough that ist for me not to like him."

Reis stared for a moment at him, then turned and walked out of the shelter. His cheeks were red with anger or perhaps, only the heat from the furnace. He didn't go back for the rest of the day.

Master Altschmer stared at him often after that, his eyes following Reis wherever he went. It was unnerving. With Master Greutter he was the same, joking, talking in low German tones. But when he saw Reis he stared and one day went out of his way to offer him a piece of roasted meat. Reis stared back wanting to refuse, but he didn't. Instead he found himself taking the roasted chunk and popping it in his mouth, nodding to the man who nodded in return. Greutter made a coarse comment and Altschmer turned unexpectedly on him, speaking harshly. Though Reis couldn't understand a word, he felt certain that Master Altschmer had told his fellow worker off.

Several more men came down with the ague including Master Haring, principal digger, so Ralph Lane conferring with Thomas Hariot, stopped the work temporarily and quarantined those who were sick. Delighted with such a holiday, Reis, Jeremie and Hugh, for Master Snelling was also sick, went off to the river's edge to fish. Hugh lost interest right away, but Jeremie and Reis managed to catch some fine fat fish and sent Hugh with them back to the camp. Then he and Jeremie went trudging off into the woodlands to see if any rabbits had been caught in the snares.

The trees and brush were thick and quite overgrown. It was hard going and Reis wondered how far they should walk before turning back. But they found one rabbit in a snare with its neck broken and decided to walk just a little further. Jeremie strung the dead creature over his shoulder and thumped his chest.

"Mighty hunter," he cackled, then darted away. Reis grinned. It was good to spend some time away from the furnace and its unbearable heat. The woods were chilly and damp; last night the first frost had cast a white sheen over everything. He shivered a little, wishing he had thought to wear his thick jacket.

"Where are you?" he called out to Jeremie but there was no reply. "Come you, 'tis time to go back," but again not a sound from his young friend.

Reis frowned. It was getting late and perhaps Dougham was looking for him. He called out to Jeremie and thought he heard a sound. Heading in the direction, he found himself torn by briars and scratched upon his already blistered arms. He gave a small cry of pain, then stumbled into a clearing to see Jeremie held in the vise-like grasp of a painted Savage.

Reis gasped. The Savage was standing there boldly, one arm around Jeremie's waist, the other around his neck. Jeremie's eyes were large and frightened beyond all reasoning. He couldn't call out for the wind was being squeezed from him. Reis saw Jeremie's eyes roll back and watched him slump over. The Savage gave a grunt and released his body to the ground. Jeremie lay in a small crumpled heap, no more than the dead rabbit still hanging from his shoulder. The Savage grabbed the rabbit and turned, stepping silently into the trees. When Reis blinked his eyes again he was gone. Reis felt his bowels turn to water. But he ran, instead, to his friend and shook him.

"Wake up, wake up."

What would he do if Jeremie were dead? How would he tell the men at the camp what had happened? Would the Savage have killed him, too? Jeremie began to cough and moan, then suddenly sat up. He looked around with huge eyes.

"Is he gone?"

Reis nodded.

"What happened?"

"I was running and before I knew it, I felt myself grabbed from behind. He was choking me to death."

Reis pulled Jeremie to his feet.

"'Tis best we get out of here. He may be back. But I think he wanted your rabbit, that's all."

Jeremie was close to tears. He wiped his eyes furiously and rubbed his nose on his sleeve.

"Come," said Reis, pulling him back toward their camp. "Come away now, lest there be others."

The thought that there might be yet more Savages lurking

in the trees caused Jeremie to sniff even louder. Reis tugged and tugged until he began to move. Reis kept glancing back into the thickness of the brambles. Was that a painted figure he saw darting behind a tree? Or was there one over in the grove just beyond that boulder? A sudden fear surged through him; he felt it coursing his veins, 'run, run fast,' and so they both began to race toward the camp. As they ran Reis imagined the arrow drawn back in the bow, the swift projectile speeding toward him, even now penetrating his body. He stumbled and almost fell, picked himself up and, dragging Jeremie, flew all the way back to the encampment.

"Ho now, what's this? What has startled our apprentices so that they run into our camp as if another bear were after them?"

"Perchance they saw a lion, or maybe an elephant?"

Reis was gasping for breath.

"It was... it was...."

"A Savage," cried Jeremie. "A Savage with paint on his face. He grabbed me and strangled me."

At this the men jumped up. Master Hariot came running from the furnace shelter.

"Quick, boy, tell us again," called Master Haring from his sick bed, rising up on one elbow.

"A Savage, say you?"

"Indeed, sir, one with stripes running down his face. He was holding Jeremie and choking him."

The men began to gather in small group, conversing wildly. Some ran for their muskets and powder. Master Haring, claiming not to be sick any more, rose and pulled on his boots. Hugh Salter ran to hide in Master Snelling's tent. Jeremie and

Reis found themselves the center of attention and Jeremie, feeling safe amidst all the men, began expanding upon his tale. By the time he'd finished, his story included twenty Indians and a fire dance. Master Hariot fetched Ralph Lane who, by now, had heard the commotion. Master Lane immediately called the soldiers under his command into action and a detail of harquebusiers, with their sturdy muskets, were sent forth to scour the woodlands. Sentries were posted around the entire area and several perimeter fires were built and kept burning through the night.

Ralph Lane questioned Reis and Jeremie both, and the latter recanted his tale of so many and the fact that it was just one solitary native made the men breathe more easily.

"But vere there ist one, others there are," Master Greutter's voice came loud and clear and the men murmured their agreement.

"Perhaps he was alone," Dougham ventured, "perhaps he was hunting only for food far from his camp. He took, after all, the rabbit the boy had."

Master Greutter's answer was biting and harsh.

"A rabbit now, then the boy, later us. Unless Master Gaunse thinks he ist safe because he, too, ist a heathen among us?"

Dougham's eyes flashed, Master Greutter glared at him and Reis thought the two might have come to blows, except that Ralph Lane came in between and ordered Dougham to return to his hut and Master Greutter to his. Reis followed Dougham and willed his heart to stop beating so fast. A meeting of the men was swiftly called to order.

CHAPTER 9
THE SEARCH PARTY

RALPH LANE'S SOLDIERS tramped through brush and thicket around the place where Jeremie and Reis saw the Indian, but came back foot-sore and weary to say they'd found nothing.

"We crossed the entire area. There were no signs of one, nor many."

Master Lane questioned Jeremie again, then called Reis over.

"Describe this Savage to me."

Reis closed his eyes for a moment. He pictured the man holding fast to Jeremie, his hold slowly suffocating the boy, his eyes bright with anger…, no, it could have been hunger. He was lean and his ribs showed. His skin was dark and his hair black and flowing. Upon his faces were stripes of yellow and red.

"That's all I remember, sir," Reis said.

Ralph Lane looked harshly at him.

"Did you see others, Think, boy."

Reis shook his head. There had been no others, at least none that were not in his imagination.

"How did you get away? Was there a struggle?"

Reis wondered what story Jeremie had told this great military man to impress him.

"There was no struggle. Jeremie fainted and the Savage grabbed the dead rabbit and ran back into the woods."

Ralph Lane leaned back and ran his fingers through his hair.

"There was no attack?"

Reis shook his head.

"You're sure of that?"

Master Lane called Thomas Hariot over to discuss the matter. Reis saw them conferring in serious tones. He walked over to Jeremie, where Hugh was hanging on his every word.

"What did you do when he drew his knife?"

Reis grabbed Jeremie.

"Such tales will get you in trouble," he said angrily.

"He could have had a knife, you know. Maybe it was hidden...."

"Well, he didn't use it on you."

Master Hariot beckoned to Reis to join his discussion with Lane.

"We're concerned," he said, "for trouble with the natives is not what we wish."

"I think he was only hungry. I think he wanted Jeremie's rabbit, the one we took from the snare. He could have killed Jeremie, but he didn't."

Ralph Lane furrowed his brows. Reis boldly asked his question.

"Master Hariot, I thought the natives had welcomed the expedition last year. Isn't that true? Why would they wish to harm us?"

"When Amadas and Barlow's men came in 1584, this Secotan tribe was friendly enough. But there was trouble that arose soon after and some of the soldiers were killed. Ralph Lane thinks these may be the same as those before, led by one called Wingina, who now calls himself Pemisapan. There is always the possibility of trouble. We hope to trade with them for their copper, and that they'll tell us their sources. Now that the one ran away, who knows what stories he may tell."

"Only of two very frightened apprentices, I should think."

Master Hariot gave a wry smile.

"Were you frightened?"

Reis wanted to say "No," but both men were staring at him.

"I was most frightened. And when Jeremie dropped to the ground, I thought for certain the Savage had killed him."

"Was he wearing any decorations of copper, perhaps around his neck or his wrist?"

"I saw nothing, I was...."

Thomas Hariot gave a small nod of his head and Reis walked away. Master Amadas, who had visited the Virginia lands in 1584 one year ago and had volunteered with great eagerness to accompany Sir Grenville's expedition this year, went to join the other two.

Reis sought out Hugh and Jeremie again. They were eating and he joined them, suddenly realizing how famished he was. It was all too frightening for Hugh, whose mouth kept trembling at the corners.

"What if they come into our camp? What if they creep up in the middle of the night. We'll be killed in our sleep!"

Jeremie nodded his head wisely.

"He was a fearsome sort, that's for certain...." Then he saw Reis staring at him. "Well, I didn't get to see his face, actually, he was behind me and holding me fast."

Hugh was trembling even more.

"I told Master Ralph he was probably hungry and after the rabbit. If he had wanted to kill Jeremie, he would have done so right away."

But Hugh was not to be comforted. H rose from his place and went to Master Snelling's tent, there to bed most probably, Reis thought.

Jeremie tugged on Reis's arm.

"Perhaps the two Savages we had with us were in league with them."

Reis knew he was talking about Manteo and Wanchese, the two chiefs who had returned from England as part of this expedition, having been brought there in 1584 by Amadas and Barlowe. He shook his head.

"They were friendly to us," he corrected Jeremie. "And besides, they've long since returned to their own people on Croatoan Island."

"Maybe that's why they left, knowing we would be attacked."

Reis laughed.

"I don't know where you get these ideas which fill your head. I overheard Master Lane praising Manteo for his helpfulness. Why would he wish to harm us? And if he knew of any attacks, surely he would have warned us all."

Reis remembered the two Savages on the long voyage across the mighty sea. They had kept to themselves, speaking only with Master Hariot and that, to learn more English and

to teach him their Croatoan tongue. They were both imposing figures, dark-skinned and muscular, with many shells and
decorations about them, and painted symbols upon their bare
shoulders. When The Tyger laid anchor, they had watched the
men construct the settlement then spoke to Sir Thomas in low
voices, after which Wanchese took his canoe and set sail for
his island home to the south while Manteo stayed and assisted
in some early explorations.

Master Lane called a meeting of all the captains and men
at arms. They conferred long into the night and the conclusion was reached, Reis learned later, that an exploratory party
would be sent north to search for signs of these Indians and
see what supplies of copper they might have or know about.
It would be a small group, possibly eight to ten men, with no
soldiers to alarm them, and with many trinkets of glass, beads
and dolls to barter for their copper jewelry. Reis wanted to go
desperately. His heart was racing with the idea for, dangerous
though it was, it was better by far than staying at the camp
listening to Hugh and Jeremie whine about things, or cleaning
boots and fetching firewood. He ran to ask Master Dougham
if he might accompany them.

Surprisingly enough Master Dougham, after pondering
the idea at some length, decided that it would be a good experience for him and besides, he could help carry some of the
equipment.

"But it is of grave danger, for who knows what confronta-
tions we may face."

Reis hoped fervently that Ralph Lane would grant him
permission to go. He watched all day and the next for a sign
from Dougham that he was allowed, but his master said not a

word, just busied himself with the gathering of equipment he felt he would need.

The men for the expedition north were picked carefully. Dougham would go, of course, for his skill in recognizing pure copper when he saw it. There would be Hans Altschmer to help with the determination of its purity by smelting. Then Thomas Hariot for his knowledge as a translator and John White, to draw the maps according to his skill. Master Lane would command the group and Philip Amadas, Edward Stafford and Captain Vaughan were to come, along with Masters Greutter and Haring for their strength. Master Lane changed his mind at the last moment and added two harque-busiers, a young soldier by the name of Valentine Beale, and another for protection. Added to the final list was the name of Reis Courtney, as bearer of such equipment and goods as he could carry. Reis was elated.

They were to head northward to explore the Chesapeake Baye, to map out the coastal regions there and try to find both a deep-water harbor and rich veins of copper. Instructions were given for maps to be drawn and charted. They would stay the winter months and return when their work was completed. The trinkets of beads and colored glass, and the dolls fashioned with wool hair and glass eyes, were for any Indian children of the warriors they might meet.

"'Tis a known fact that the Savages prize their children and will warm to those who offer them gifts."

They would leave two days hence, so Reis was kept busy sorting and packing. Outwardly he rejoiced, inwardly he was filled with a strange trepidation, a combination of wariness and outright fear at what they might encounter. The tales of torture and savagery among the northern tribes were well-known to those Englishmen who had traversed these lands before them; captured Spaniards had only served to heighten fear by adding their own tales of ferocity.

"I'm glad it's you and not me who is going," remarked Hugh while watching Reis pack. "I wouldn't venture forth into unknown territory. This be enough for me and at least we have the soldiers to guard us."

Reis shrugged, though Hugh's words weighed heavily on his mind.

Jeremie said, "Well, I for one, wish I were going. It'll be a great adventure and it doesn't scare me."

Reis thought of Jeremie's eyes rolling back in his head as the Savage squeezed tighter. He grinned.

"Then ask Master Lane if you might go as well," he suggested.

But when Jeremie approached their leader, the latter shook his head vehemently and forbid him. Jeremie sulked all day but Reis thought it a good decision; Jeremie was, after all, only ten. Reis kept out of everyone's way during the rest of the preparations, busying himself with cleaning the equipment, packing the instruments, weights and measures that Dougham would need on such a long trip. He thought it best not to be underfoot, but kept his eyes and ears open so he could learn as much as he could about their journey. He hoped fervently that Master Lane wouldn't change his mind and decide to strike his name from the list.

CHAPTER 10
THE JOURNEY NORTH

THEY MOVED OUT of the encampment amidst cheers of good luck from those remaining. The men wore thick garments for the nights were chill and as they headed North, Master Hariot said there would be a greater chance of snow. All the men were weighted down with equipment and some carried tents which could easily be pitched as shelters. Reis was so loaded that he staggered under his packs. It wasn't long before his shoulders ached mightily and the ropes cut into his arms and chest. But he said not a word, for to complain would be to admit weakness. In disgust, Master Dougham might order him to turn around and follow the trail back to the main camp.

By the time they stopped for the night, Reis thought his back was surely broken. His calf muscles burned with fire and he shivered both from cold and tension. He was thankful when Master Amadas finally called a halt to their walking and they made rough camp at the river's edge. They would follow the Chowan River north to where it joined the Blackwater, then northeast again, close to the Chesapeake lands.

Their camp was rude and makeshift and everyone was too tired to fish or lay a snare, so they ate the few provisions they'd brought. Tomorrow and all the days thereafter they would have to live off the land. Dougham, as usual, kept himself apart from the others, his crude tent pitched near the trees. Reis waited for his master to invite him to share sleeping quarters, at the ready with his rolled blanket. But Dougham made no such offer and Reis contented himself by staying close to the fire's light and warmth. Near the fire he felt safer but strangely enough, he longed to be at Dougham's side listening to his stories of copper and gold, hoping for yet another Jewish tale, how God had chosen the Jews for His very own people and why He had done so. Right at that moment his master, no doubt, was saying his prayers.

Reis tried to remember the strange sounding Hebrew words, *"Baruch atah Adonai...,"* but he forgot the rest and sleep overcame him.

They were up at the dawn's breaking and packed quickly. The fire was quenched and soon they were on the move. Reis's stomach rumbled and groaned in protest. He saw no signs of anyone stopping for the midday meal either and he thought, 'If I don't eat soon I will lose my senses.' It was not until the sun was way low in the sky that Master Amadas called a halt and they built a second crude camp. The men were footsore as well, and grumbling from the emptiness in their stomachs. Ralph Lane sent Valentine Beale and Master Greutter to find a deer or perhaps, some rabbits. Reis was sent to the river's edge to try his skill at fishing. He was lucky and caught three fat ones. The men greeted his return most enthusiastically and soon a roaring fire was going and the fish, cleaned and gutted, were skewered above it. Master Greutter's voice hailed them from the forest's edge and he and Valentine Beale strode into camp holding two plump hares and shouldering a very young doe.

Reis felt comforted by the sight and sound of these hearty men. Master Amadas professed to know the country, having traveled here the prior year and he was discussing which route they should follow with Thomas Hariot. Captain Vaughan was arguing the merits of bronze for use in cannons.

"We prefer bronze," he stated emphatically, "for it is much stronger."

"We must first find the copper," said Dougham in his quiet voice.

"But that ist vy ve haf you, mein fine Master Gaunse," Greutter's voice was full of sarcasm. "You are the expert, ist not so?"

Dougham nodded slightly.

"If you say so, Master Greutter."

"I say," said Master Greutter, "und vat I say ist true, you are the expert. For that ve tolerate your presence among us, though ve could find this copper by ourselves, ich bin mir sicher."

"Enough," added Master Haring, coming over and giving Greutter a look. The latter moved further away from Dougham to the other side.

"Never mind him," Haring told Dougham. "He ist bad-mannered, that ist all."

"More than that," muttered Dougham and got up, walking back to his favorite place near the trees.

Reis got up to relieve himself. He was turning to go when

he heard a rustling in the brush. His heart leaped in his chest. A Savage, it was another Savage come to grab him and cut his throat or throttle him, the way the other had tried to do with Jeremie. His mouth was so dry he couldn't call out nor say a single word. He wanted to run and warn the others but....

"It's me," whispered a small voice.

"Who?"

"Me, Jeremie," and from behind the very bush where Reis was standing there stepped his young friend. Jeremie's clothing was torn and his face and hands scratched. Reis grabbed him, he was so relieved.

"What are you doing here? I thought you were a hostile come to attack me."

"I'm sore afraid." Jeremie's voice was low and fearful. "I've been following you ever since you left the camp, staying out of sight. Please don't tell them I'm here."

"Master Lane will surely be angry that you followed without his permission."

"I know."

Jeremie hung his head, looking miserable. "But I couldn't stay. I just had to come. I don't think it's fair that I couldn't come."

"I shall tell Master Lane you're here."

"No, don't!"

Jeremie grabbed his arm. "If you do, he'll surely send me back."

"He can't send you back, silly. Now that you're here he would never let you go back alone. It's far too dangerous."

Reis paused to look at Jeremie.

"And how did you find us? Where did you sleep?"

"I followed your trail. And I slept as close to you as I dared. It was terribly cold and damp. And I'm starving."

Reis went back to the fire and returned to where Jeremie was hiding. He handed him some pieces of fish and meat.

"That's all there is, so eat and be done. Then you must come with me into camp."

"I dare not. They will all laugh at me. No, I'll just stay out of sight and follow you. You can bring me food. And perhaps," he shivered, "a blanket to wrap around myself."

Jeremie looked so frightened and anxious that Reis didn't have the heart to tell on him. He nodded slightly in agreement, then slipped back to camp. When he returned to Jeremie, he handed him the blanket.

"'Tis my own. I'll have to beg one from the others. Now don't say a word and stay close."

"I will," Jeremie promised, nodding his head up and down. "I'm too afraid not to."

Reis looked at his friend.

"I'll have to think on this. I won't say anything... yet."

Jeremie wrapped the blanket around himself and settled down in a small heap.

"Don't tell, remember, you promised."

Reis bit his lip as he went back to the others. It was danger-ous for Jeremie to be sleeping out there alone. Suppose there were Savages scouting the area? Suppose there were wolves? But Jeremie had made him promise. And there was always the chance Ralph Lane would, indeed, send him packing. And maybe he'd be so angry he'd send Reis as well. He decided to keep quiet for a while, then talk privately to Dougham. Maybe his master could then persuade the others to let Jeremie stay.

It was the best plan he could think of at the moment. He borrowed a blanket from Master Haring, who didn't seem to mind, and settled down for the night. The air was chill and he slept fitfully, hearing strange noises throughout the night. He wondered how Jeremie was faring on the far side of the brush, curled in his blanket and hoping no hostiles were around to grab him.

When he awoke the next morning, Reis looked over toward the bushes wondering if he could spot Jeremie. There was no sign of him. Perhaps he'd been dreaming after all, imagining the whole thing. Uncle Allyn had always called him "the dreamer," and he'd oft been chastised for standing with his head in the clouds instead of working, just like poor Hugh with Master Snelling.

"Dreaming of what?" Uncle had asked but he'd said nothing.

"Dreaming of his fortune," laughed his cousins, taunting him further for his foolish ways. That was when he'd resolved never to dream again and to make sure he did what he was told. But the dreams, if not stopping his work, kept swirling round and round inside his head. 'I be a dreamer,' he thought, 'dreaming of getting out of here and to a world full of adventure.' It was his dreams that had made him bold enough to step up to Dougham Gaunse that fateful morn in Surrey. And here he was!

But it was silly to think that Jeremie would have followed their tracks and slept alone for two nights. Reis shook his head to clear the cobwebs. No, he'd been dreaming, all right, of that he was sure! He rolled up the blanket and handed it to Master Haring, who shook his head.

"If yours ist lost, then use this. It freezes at night," only he said, "nacht" instead of night. Reis nodded, for he was beginning to understand some of the German words.

He strapped the packs and equipment on, then realized he hadn't eaten breakfast. There was only bread and stale biscuits and some greasy meat left, but it would suffice. He grabbed an extra biscuit and piece of meat, just in case... just in case....

"You are hungry?" Master Dougham commented.

Reis nodded and walked slowly over to the brush line. If he'd dreamt the whole thing, then nothing would be there. If not, Jeremie would be starving again. There was nothing behind the bush. Reis walked around a little more searching for a sign of his friend. Master Dougham called him over.

"Come now, we are leaving."

Reis's heart skipped a beat. Had the wolves grabbed Jeremie in the middle of the night? Had a hostile seized him? But he heard just then a faint "pssst!" and walked further. Jeremie was crouched behind a thick clump of bushes.

"I wasn't dreaming...," Reis began. Jeremie stared at him but didn't say a word, for he had grabbed the food from Reis's hand and stuffed it all in his mouth.

"We're leaving," he whispered. Jeremie nodded.

"Stay as close as you can without being seen."

Again Jeremie nodded.

"I will talk with Dougham. Perhaps he'll help us."

They traveled until dark, not stopping for a break until the sun was sinking behind the low clouds on the horizon. A few flakes of snow were drifting down and Reis shivered. He thought constantly about poor Jeremie trudging behind, wondering if he could keep up, wondering if he'd changed his mind and turned back to the main encampment.

"You be lost in thought, boy," called Master Hariot coming over and standing in front of him. "What can be on your mind?"

But when Reis didn't say anything, he added,

"Perchance you should have stayed back with the others. 'Tis a long and wearisome journey for a young boy."

"No, sir," Reis shook his head. "I can keep up. I wanted to come with you."

"Indeed you did," smiled Master Hariot. "For I saw how you kept pestering Dougham."

Reis turned red again. How childish he must have seemed to this great man and the others, a foolish lad who whined to be taken along. He slipped out of his packs and started helping to set up the rude shelters. They shouldn't think him a child or a burden. He pitched tents and hammered stakes until blisters popped on his hands. When at length the camp was rough and ready, he went to gather firewood for the night. Master Hariot watched him with an amused look. Even Dougham Gaunse tried not to smile.

"Your apprentice is full of great zeal tonight," Sir Thomas remarked to Dougham.

"What did you say to him?"

"Nothing, only that perhaps he might wish he'd remained and not ventured forth with us."

Dougham nodded.

"A hard worker he is. I have no complaints that he comes with us."

"He will grow to manhood quickly in this wild land."

Dougham grunted and turned once more to his notes.

"I still wait to see signs of ore, but none so far."

"Captain Vaughn has scouted ahead and reports a vein that might contain some copper."

Dougham turned with an expectant look. "At last," he said.

Reis wrapped himself in his blanket and listened to the howls of wolves in the distance and the low hooting of owls as they swooped to catch mice. He shivered continually until his own body's heat warmed the air under the blanket. He was still hungry and he thought about Jeremie alone and cold, going without supper. As he drifted off to sleep his last two thoughts were of his friend huddled out in the trees, and that he was wrong for not telling the others about him.

CHAPTER 11
TROUBLE BREWING

MASTER GREUTTER WAS about to pick a fight with Dougham. It had been brewing for several days. Everyone knew it and oft times, Master Lane was forced to keep Greutter busy scouting ahead with Captain Vaughan and Valentine Beale, while Dougham walked alone notebook in hand, scribbling furiously all the while.

Reis kept as close to Dougham as his master would allow. Whenever they stopped, Dougham would go off toward the trees and squat down, writing and drawing his diagrams. At those times, Reis would slip out of his heavy packs and stretch his aching muscles. Then he'd run to fetch Master Dougham water, bread or vegetables, whatever he wanted. Sometimes Dougham accepted what he offered; other times he waved him away with an angry hand.

It was hard to figure out what his master really wanted. Mainly to be left alone to write his notes and draw his pictures, Reis thought. The pictures were always of furnaces, types of ore, smelting procedures. The notes were written in languages Reis couldn't read other than English, sometimes

Latin (for Master Hariot had told him that). Sometimes Dougham wrote in a peculiar script with strange symbols. And that, Sir Thomas had added, was probably Hebrew, the language of the Jews. Reis thought it wondrous that Dougham could write in so many different languages. He must be a very clever man, though from the looks of him one couldn't ever tell. He wore his long black cape always and a hat which was pulled down low upon his forehead. His beard was black and bushy and his hair curled long by the sides of his ears, though he usually kept it hidden.

"You think I am strange?" Dougham asked one late afternoon when he caught Reis staring at him after he'd removed his hat for a few moments. Reis turned flaming red.

"Well?"

"No, sir... I just... well...."

"You stumble over your words, boy, like a child. Speak what is on your mind, for others always do."

"Your hair is long and curling by your ears," Reis finally blurted out. He could have bitten off his tongue. He waited for his master to get angry, but Dougham smiled instead.

"This is the custom of my people," he finally replied, "to wear our hair long at the sides. These are called *Payis*. Do they offend you?"

"No, sir. It's just different."

"Thou shalt not round off the peya of your head."

Reis didn't understand the symbolism at all. Dougham put his hat back on, tucking the long strands under so they couldn't be seen. He waved him away then and turned back to his notes. Reis was sure he had, indeed, offended him and made pains to guard his tongue, his obdurate tongue which seemed to have a mind of its own, always getting him into trouble with his master.

One evening when they had finished eating and all were still hungry for game was getting scarce, Master Greutter rose from where he'd been sitting and strode across the ground to Dougham Gaunse sitting on an outcrop of boulder. Dougham paid him no heed, which annoyed Master Greutter to the point where he leaned over and snatched the notebook from Dougham's hands.

"Alvays writing, alvays so busy," said Erhart Greutter's voice, loud and booming. Master Hariot sprang instantly to the alert.

Dougham looked up without saying a word. He held out his hand for the notebook. Greutter began thumbing through it turning page after page.

"Vat ist this writing? I can not read a thing."

"It is English, or Latin, or Hebrew," replied Dougham. "It depends what is my fancy for the day."

"Not German? That I can read."

Greutter put the book close to his nose.

"It smells... it smells...," he began.

"The only thing you smell," Master Dougham said after a thoughtful moment, "is the stink of your own clothes."

Master Greutter threw the notebook on the ground, pulled back his fist and knocked Dougham Gaunse right off the boulder. Reis gasped and waited to see what Dougham would do. So did the others except for Master Hariot, who walked swiftly over and grabbed Greutter's arm.

"Enough," commanded Thomas Hariot, clearly angry.

Dougham pulled himself to his feet and brushed the dirt

from his cape. He held out his hand again and this time, with Sir Thomas glaring at him, Greutter thrust the book back.

"To your place," said Master Hariot and Greutter grudgingly obeyed. He kept glancing over his shoulder at Dougham, who had resumed his seat upon the boulder and was once again calmly writing. When Reis went over he saw the big red mark on his master's cheek where Greutter had hit him.

"Are you... all right?"

His master's eyes flashed, the way they had flashed when he'd reminded Reis of his own words about Christ.

"Leave me."

Reis went alone to the edge of the woods hoping to find Jeremie and give him some leftover food. He found the boy huddled under a bush, ravenously hungry. Jeremie grabbed the scraps and began devouring them.

"I told you there'd be trouble," he whispered with his mouth full. It was hard to understand his words. "I saw the whole thing. Now your master will cast a spell over us all, but especially over Master Greutter."

"What are you talking about?"

"They cast spells," he hissed, "against people they don't like."

"Who told you that?"

"The others. They're just waiting for your master to turn Greutter into a bat or a spider, just like a warlock."

Reis frowned. Jeremie seemed so intense, how could he believe such nonsense?

"Hurry up and finish," he said, "I have to go back."

"... or worm turds," Jeremie continued.

"That's ridiculous...," Reis started to say. Jeremie tugged on his arm.

"It's true. They do that all the time. And they can become invisible, don't you know. One moment they're there, the next gone...."

Reis turned to go.

"Is there any more?" Jeremie whispered.

Reis shook his head. Jeremie wrapped the blanket tighter around him.

"I'm freezing," he shivered. "Can you get another blanket?"

Reis walked away, his cheeks burning. It pained him to think of what the others were saying about his master. Spells indeed! It was more talk of witchery, no doubt led by Master Greutter. Reis clenched his fists, wishing that Dougham had taken his own swing at the German's face. Or better yet, that Reis was older and bigger so he could do so himself. He bumped right into Ralph Lane.

"Watch yourself, lad, for your eyes are not fixed upon your destination."

"Sorry, Master Lane."

"And what were you so engrossed in, so deep in thought about?"

Reis shook his head, not wanting to talk to this great man about Dougham and what had just happened. Master Lane frowned.

"I saw what Greutter did," he remarked. "'Tis of no consequence."

"No consequence," Reis blurted out. "To hit someone...?"

"These are good men, but rough in their ways. They will knock a few heads about at times but all are professional. We have but two purposes, to find metals for England's good and to put the fear of Almighty God into the Savages so they will not trouble us further."

Reis went back to his place by the fire. When he next looked, Dougham was gone from the boulder and nowhere in sight. He went to Dougham's tent and took an extra blanket, slipped back and handed it to Jeremie.

"You forgot more food," the boy whispered.

In the middle of the night Reis awoke suddenly. A light snow was falling and he was chilled to the bone. The fire had died down and none had arisen to kindle it. Reis hesitated for a few minutes before getting reluctantly out of his blanket. He gathered some wood together and heaped it on the smoldering embers. Within a few seconds the tinder had caught fire and flames began licking the edges of the wood. From nearby a man stirred and Reis heard him whisper, "Gut job, boy."

It was Master Haring's voice. Reis piled more wood on, feeding the hunger of the fire until it was roaring. Light from the dancing flames cast orange and red shadows on the figures of the sleeping men. He saw Master Haring settle himself down again. But Reis couldn't sleep. He had to find Dougham and see for himself that his master was all right. Wrapping the blanket around him he went to the boulder where he'd last seen Dougham. Then he walked slowly toward the tree line, watching that the shadows might not jump out and attack him. Demons and witches were known to do that. He thought of fetching Jeremie and bringing him to his master. Perhaps Dougham would help overcome Master Lane's anger when he saw the boy had disobeyed his orders. But then he decided to leave him sleeping buried within his blankets, warm enough while Reis's fingers and toes were freezing so badly they ached. He heard the low hooting of an owl, then the chatter of some other night creature. Reis walked a little further and began to pray, some half-forgotten prayer remembered from his mother or maybe his aunt, about keeping his spirit safe from harm. Something brushed against his face and he almost cried out. He had walked into a low hanging branch. He saw the witches' yellow eyes peeking out from behind the trees.

Arms surrounded his body and pulled him down. He wanted to shriek but a hand covered his mouth.

"And you are up to what, my fine apprentice? Sent by Master Greutter to spy on me?"

"Indeed not, master...."

He could hardly breathe, he was so frightened.

"Perhaps to steal my notes to give to him. What has he offered you? Silver when we find some? Gold to carry home to your uncle? Perhaps something simpler and more important, meat from the next kill to fill your belly?"

Reis felt the tears unexpectedly sting his eyelids. Could his master think so little of him? He didn't know what to say.

"Your silence tells me I speak truth, boy. You had best be gone before I lose my temper with you."

"I would steal nothing from you," Reis said urgently. "Nothing. Were I starving, or dying upon the cross...."

He stopped abruptly.

"Not a good analogy, boy." Dougham's voice was harsh and biting. "Come you to spy upon me? Or to tell the others of the strange incantations your master utters here in the woods? *Never greet a stranger in the night, for he may be a demon.*"

"Master...," Reis said miserably. "Indeed, no such thing. I came to see how you are, that's all."

Dougham's tone softened just a little.

"And what do you see?"

"A man alone and cold sitting in the middle of a forest. Come back to the fire's warmth and let me get you something to eat."

"A tempting thought but no, not tonight."Reis sat down on the ground next to him, wrapping the blanket tighter around him. The cold was penetrating and he wondered how Dougham managed not to freeze. As if reading his mind, Dougham said wryly,

"Jews don't feel the cold, know you, boy. We drink the blood of others and it keeps us warm." He stared quizzically at Reis. "You believe that?'

Reis shook his head.

"Well, that is good. For I believe it not myself, though all around seem to."

"Master, why does Master Greutter hate the Jews so much?'

Dougham sighed. He rubbed his hands together and Reis saw him shiver.

"'Tis not from the cold I shake but from the hatred of others, hatred for my people, the Jews, throughout all history."

"You said Our Lord and Savior, Jesus Christ, was a Jew?"

"Indeed, from the House of David, King of Israel. Born a Jew and died one as well."

"Why did the Jews kill Him, their own Savior?"

"The high priests of the temple turned their backs on Him. They betrayed Him to the Romans."

"Why is He not your Savior as well as ours?"

Dougham shook his head.

"Christ was a great prophet, one of God's chosen to lead us by word and deed. But not the Messiah, for He is yet to come."

Reis tried to comprehend it all. Christ was a Jew but to the Jews, not the Son of God, only a prophet.

"If Christ isn't the Messiah, then... then...."

Dougham sighed heavily.

"He is not yet come to us, though we wait and pray...."

Just then a loud voice came booming through the trees.

"I followed you, boy, und let's see vat you hast led me to."

CHAPTER 12
MASTER GREUTTER

LOOKING BACK IN memory, Reis played the scene over and over in his mind. Master Greutter marched right up to Dougham Gaunse and grabbed him by the collar of his cape. He tore the notebook from his hands and flung it on the ground. Reis was too stunned to move at first. Then Master Greutter's giant hands began closing around Dougham's throat.

Dougham was able to duck to one side, thus loosening the larger man's grip. But in his movements he exposed the chain and star that he wore around his neck and always kept hidden. Greutter's eyes fastened upon the gleam of silver and he ripped it quickly from Dougham's neck.

"Vat ist this?" he roared. "A pagan symbol?"

Without thought Reis flung himself upon the German, kicking and punching him wildly. Greutter roared again and swung his fist right into Reis's jaw. Everything went black.

When he came to he saw both Masters Hariot and Haring holding fast to Greutter, pinning his arms to his side, while Ralph Lane and Valentine Beale, harquebuser at the ready, came striding onto the scene.

"Take this man," Lane commanded, nodding at Greutter, and Valentine Beale pointed his firearm and led him away. Master Hariot picked up Dougham's notes and handed them silently back to him, Dougham straightened his cape and brushed the muck from his notebook.

"I will have none of this," bellowed Ralph Lane in great anger. "What precipitated such an argument?"

Dougham didn't answer but walked silently past Master Lane back in the direction of the camp. Lane glanced at Hariot, who shook his head. Then he spoke to Reis.

"What do you know, boy?"

"Not much, sir. Master Greutter started it."

Ralph Lane muttered something indistinguishable, then motioned Reis away. As he walked back into the fire's light Reis felt the tremendous ache in his jaw. His whole mouth hurt and when he poked his fingers inside, two teeth were loosened. He went down to the river's edge and splashed the icy water on his face. It helped only a little. By the time he got back to his sleeping place, both Ralph Lane and Thomas Hariot were back and Greutter was nowhere to be seen.

"Let him rest the night under Beale's guard. Perhaps that will cool him off."

The next morn Reis could hardly open his mouth, his jaw ached so much. He thought perhaps that the German's blow had broken the bone. The pain rose and fell in waves and he left his breakfast. Dougham Gaunse called him over and examined him. His master's touch was quick, but gentle.

"You will live. No bones broken."

"And what of you?" Reis blurted out, though it hurt to talk.

"A few bruises but I will heal." He sighed. "He has still what belongs to me."

"What will you do?"

"Ask him to give it back."

For the briefest moment Reis thought he saw a faint smile play around the corners of Dougham's mouth. But then his master's eyes grew hard and cold.

"For this is what we Jews have always faced, you see, boy. Hatred such as Greutter's cannot long be hidden away. It surfaces and we become its target. Others hear and sheep follow sheep."

"Master Dougham," Reis started to say.

"Tend to your business and leave me now. I must think on things."

Dougham turned his back on Reis and walked away. The atmosphere in the group was tense. Hans Altschmer was arguing with Thomas Hariot, asking why Greutter was under guard. Master Haring was talking with Philip Amadas, keeping his voice low so none could hear. Reis kept working his jawbone, his primary concern for the moment while Dougham, upon his return, began gathering his possessions.

"What say you, Master Yougham," Ralph Lane said, using the name he always called him by. "Are you planning to leave us now?"

"Where I am unwelcome is not the place for me. I will take my packs and my apprentice and together we will return to the encampment."

"I hope not," said Master Hariot coming over. "For you're needed here, Dougham, as well you know."

Dougham shrugged and kept packing. He nodded to Reis.

"Load up now."

Reis didn't know what to do. The thought of leaving when they were so close to discovering a possible vein of copper was distressing. Yet his loyalty was to his master. He hesitated. Master Hariot called to him.

"Untie those packs, boy. Your master will soon return to his senses."

Dougham threw up his arms in disgust.

"I can not argue with you, Thomas," he said grimly. "But be forewarned, no more will I tolerate. *A little coin in a big jar makes a lot of noise.*"

Reis glanced over at Greutter, who was scowling under Valentine Beale's weapon. Thomas Hariot walked over and held out his hand to Dougham. For but a moment his master stood there, then he grasped the extended hand and they shook.

"There will be no more trouble," Hariot assured him. "And that is my word on it."

Then he and Lane went over to where Greutter was standing and were seen talking most earnestly to him. A few minutes later Greutter came back into camp.

Dougham said not a word, nor glanced in his direction but began unloading his sacks and equipment. Reis breathed a deep sigh of relief. He helped Dougham then went, without asking, to see if he could assist any of the others.

They finished their scant meal, hardly enough to break the fast of the long night, then packed for the exploration of the outcrop of rock that Captain Vaughan had reported. Perhaps they would find copper and all would be forgotten in the excitement of the discovery. Reis hoped that Jeremie would remain out of sight until he'd had a chance to speak with his master.

Captain Vaughan's rock proved a big disappointment. The promising abutment with its streaks of violet which might have yielded pure copper showed, not that valuable substance, but merely what Hariot called white copperas and alumen plumeum. The men threw up their hands in disgust and sank down upon the ground exhausted and low in spirits. Their trek had been for naught.

Master Hariot, disappointed though he was, tried to make light of the situation.

"There will be more ridges," he promised. "Captain Vaughan says this line extends for forty or fifty miles. We may yet find what we seek."

"We shall not turn back?"

"Indeed not. We're but a week into our journey. Much more to seek out and explore. Make haste now. Gather your equipment and we'll continue on."

They walked for many miles until Reis thought his legs would fall off. Deep marks cut into his shoulders from the straps of the heavy packs. Every once in a while they stopped to stretch and slip their loads. At those times, Reis skirted the edges of the woods to see if he could spot Jeremie. He hoped fervently that the boy was keeping up, for he was only ten and, like Hugh, a great complainer. Certainly the fear of being left behind would stir him to move forward with them. To turn back would have been a lonely and perilous sojourn.

This was the pattern of their days, to walk for miles and miles resting only a little, to strike a small camp and eat what they could catch in hastily laid snares or from the many streams and ponds they passed. Reis became quite adept at catching the silver fish which swam sluggishly in the cold waters. Oft times he had to break the ice which formed on the surface. The fish were slow to dart away, some of them had half-buried themselves in the muddy bottoms of the ponds. They were an easy catch. As he lay wrapped in his blanket at night, as close to the fire as he dared, he listened to the howling of wolves and the noises of strange animals in the dark. He thought often of Jeremie for it became his routine to eat only a portion of his meal then wander away to the tree line, there to seek out his young friend and give him the rest. He begged extra blankets from Masters Haring and Hariot on the pretense of feeling so cold his toes and fingers ached. He shared the blankets with Jeremie, whose toes and fingers were, no doubt, much colder than his own. But he still hadn't told anyone, nor enlisted Dougham's aid in the matter. For Dougham was becoming more and more morose and on the occasions of his conversation, given to harsh tones and quick outbursts. Reis felt certain Dougham would not speak on Jeremie's behalf to Ralph Lane.

Master Greutter kept his part of the bargain, staying far away from Dougham Gaunse. But he still hadn't returned the silver Hebrew star, though Dougham had asked him several times. Master Greutter feigned ignorance of the matter and shook his head whenever Dougham approached. It was plain to see that his master's patience was wearing thinner each day. He scribbled his notes each evening and Reis wondered what he was writing since there seemed nothing to report. Each day brought them closer to the land of the Chesepians, but the ridge they followed revealed no promising veins. One night after Reis had given Jeremie the remains of his own meal, he watched as Dougham Gaunse walked slowly over to Greutter and held out his hand.

"Vat ist this?" Greutter feigned ignorance.

"You have what belongs to me."

"Aber nein, I haf nothing."

Thomas Hariot was watching closely from the edge of the fire's light. He half-rose, but waited instead.

"The Magen David," said Dougham.

Greutter rolled his eyes to fake pretense at bewilderment. He turned to Altschmer seated next to him.

"Do you know vat ist he means?"

Master Altschmer shook his head.

"I want it back."

"I can not give vat I do not haf. Go back to your seat now."

Dougham reached forward in the glow of the flames and pulled Master Greutter to his feet. It was a brave move for the miner was taller than he.

"My Magen David," Dougham repeated slowly. "That which you stole from me."

By now Master Hariot was on his feet and so was Master Haring from the opposite side.

Greutter slapped Dougham's hands away and pushed him hard. Reis saw his master come forward again and reach deep into one of the pockets in Greutter's cape.

"Nein, nein," shouted the miner, again shoving Dougham who, this time, fell backward. But as he went down Reis saw in his hand the silver chain and star.

"You see," Dougham yelled from where he had fallen. His face was flushed and Reis had never heard his voice so raised in anger.

"You are a liar, Master Greutter, but you have been found out. The others will now see what a thief you are! *Truth is the seal of God!*"

It took two men to hold Greutter back. As it was, Valentine Beale finally had to point his firearm at the man to subdue him. Dougham Gaunse got up slowly but triumph was clearly marked upon his face.

"Vat ist that?" Master Altschmer asked. The others were crowding around, all curious to see what he held. Caught in the color of the flames, it glowed silver, red and gold.

"Jude! Jude!" growled Greutter and began muttering angrily to Altschmer.

It took Master Hariot, Ralph Lane and Captain Vaughan a time to quiet them down. Ralph Lane spoke in great anger.

"I will have no more of this," he said, glaring at both Greutter and Dougham. "We will have no name-calling here."

Master Greutter pushed the end of Beale's harquebuser to one side and stepped forward.

"If he ist not Jude, let him deny it."

From where he stood Reis watched his master slowly fasten the chain with its heavy silver star around his neck. Greutter and Altschmer began to mutter again in German. Master Lane was clearly enraged and Sir Thomas most distressed. They all waited.

Then Dougham spoke. His voice rang loud and clear.

"I deny nothing."

His eyes swept the group defiantly. "See me stand here before all of you. It is the truth Master Greutter speaks. I am a Jew. And my real name is Joachim Gans."

CHAPTER 13
JEREMIE

TWO DAYS LATER they encountered a small group of Indians led by a chief called Menatonon. He was a formidable fellow and Ralph Lane was clearly not pleased to see him. They had marched for miles along the once-promising ridge line, east and north, taking rock samples and stopping to heat the rock in crude stone furnaces wrought by Masters Greutter and Haring. The fires inside burned hot, tended by Altschmer, and the ores that pooled were tested over and over by Joachim Gans.

He made Reis call him Master Gans now and answered only to that or Joachim. He no longer went to the forest's edge to read his Holy Book of prayers but prayed within sight and sound of the others, defying them to say anything with his dark flashing eyes. Master Greutter, sarcastic as ever with the others, surprisingly held his tongue and his friend, Altschmer the smelter, worked alongside Joachim each day roasting the rock samples until they ran liquid, waiting for the Jew's instruments and measures to define their value. They pounded the copper ore into a powder, roasted this yet again and passed water through it. Water, as Joachim explained, carried away the vitriol, iron and sulfur and thus, cleansed the ore of its slag or dross.

As for Reis, he was busier than ever, helping to gather and haul the samples that Master Haring chipped and hewed from each rock face, sweating in his labor of carrying the loads down to the rough furnace. He fetched water, gathered kindling and firewood, was sent to check the streams and ponds for fish which, by now, had the good sense to bury themselves deep under the mud for the waters were icy cold.

Each evening Reis walked to the perimeter of their temporary camp and left food for his friend. But he never saw him nor spoke to him, and wondered if he were still alive and following them. The only sign was the empty plate the next morn, though it could have been scavengers eating the scraps, he had no way of knowing. When he could, he would venture all around the brush and trees seeking Jeremie, whispering his name and waiting for an answer, any sound. There was none.

Every time he thought about telling Dougham, no, it was Joachim now, his master waved him away with an impatient hand. Joachim still ate alone and wrote his notes in English, Latin or Hebrew depending, as he had said, upon his mood. Most often now they were in Hebrew, out of defiance or anger, Reis didn't know. He watched his master one day as he wrote, trying not to appear as if he were watching but seeing the strange letters formed from right to left.

It was all backwards, this Hebrew writing. And Reis could make no sense of what Master Gans wrote. There were no letters he recognized, not an "A," nor "R" for Reis's own name. Though he could write but little, nor form his letters well,

Reis could read. His Uncle Allyn had seen fit to teach him though his aunt clicked her teeth angrily whenever her husband sat him down.

"Wasting his time when he could be cleaning out the pigs or fetching wood," was all she ever said. Uncle Allyn shrugged,

"Every boy should know how to read," and just continued. Reis learned his skill from a tattered Bible and though his own father had never read nor ever shown him the Holy Book, Uncle Allyn was always spouting proverbs and such pulled from its worn pages.

"'Tis God's word," Allyn said and that became the only exposure to religion Reis had. He enjoyed sitting next to his uncle, out of the cold and muck from the pig pen. He learned fast and once, when his aunt and uncle were helping a neighbor with a birthing cow, Reis took the Book and picked out the passages he liked best, committing them to memory.

He wasn't sure he liked this new Joachim Gans, though he had greatly admired Dougham Gaunse and hung upon his every word. Joachim no longer troubled to tuck his long side hair under his hat. Every night he took his silver star and rubbed and polished it deliberately in front of the others. Thomas Hariot watched with a bemused look on his face; Ralph Lane was busy plotting his strategy should the Savages appear; John White was drawing his maps and pictures; only Greutter and Altschmer stared stonily from their place across the fire. Reis wished Joachim was not so arrogant in his ways that he angered these men. But Joachim Gans, mineral man, didn't seem to care.

When the warriors of Menatonon appeared, Reis had been away from the camp searching again for Jeremie.

"Hist," he called over and over. "Jeremie, where be you hiding? 'Tis cold and I've some food for you."

A thin hand reached out and grabbed at his ankle. Reis almost dropped the plate and the bundle of clothing he was carrying. He looked down and saw Jeremie crouched low under a prickly bramble.

"Where have ye been?" Reis asked, noting the thinness in the boy's face and his pinched and nervous look.

"There were Savages about so I kept moving. Every time you came I was hidden deep in the woods. 'Tis fearsome scary and lonely. I hear the witches."

Reis shivered. Which was worse, Savages or witches? In truth, he didn't know.

"You must come back to camp with me now," Reis insisted. "Far too dangerous it is for you to be out here all alone."

"I will tonight, I promise. For you're right, I'm frightened and the Savages seem to be moving closer."

He glanced around the woods and Reis did the same, almost expecting a painted warrior to step from the shadows. But there was nothing.

"Why don't you come now?"

Jeremie shook his head.

"Master Lane is angry, I know. I heard him yelling this morn. For sure he would send me back if he saw me."

"Not now. We've come too far for him to make you return. No, he'll yell and rant, but with us you'll stay."

Jeremie nodded and began to scramble out from the bush. Just then Reis heard a strange sound and looked up to see a group of Savages stepping from the forest into the small clearing. Jeremie must have seen them also, for he scrabbled back under the bush faster than Reis could blink an eye. The Savages hadn't seen him for they were looking over Reis's shoulder at the men and the campfire.

Reis back slowly away from the bramble bush, hoping Jeremie had the good sense to stay hidden. He kept backing as the Indians came forward until he was at the camp's edge. Only then did he take in a deep breath and realized he'd been holding it all the while. Masters Hariot and Amadas saw the Savages behind him and came forward. Master Thomas held his hand up in a greeting. He spoke in a strange language which Reis had never heard before.

"The great Menatonon, King of Choanoke," is what he said and Reis could understand only "Menatonon."

The Savage, who walked with a bad limp, spoke to Thomas Hariot at some length, none of which Reis could fathom. He watched as Ralph Lane came forward and Master Lane spoke rapidly to Hariot, who translated for Manatonon. He had four warriors with him, strong men with brown skin and feathers in their hair. They had thick cloaks of animal skin wrapped around them against the cold. Heat from their breath formed clouds in front of their faces.

The talk was loud and vigorous. From what Reis learned afterward, Menatonon warned Master Lane of plans by Wingina to attack them. Wingina, now calling himself Pemisapan, was busy gathering his warriors together to persuade them and neighboring tribes to attack the English.

"Wingina has turned hostile to us," Sir Thomas explained, clearly upset. At the end of their discussion, Ralph Lane ordered Valentine Beale to take Menatonon and his son, Skiko, prisoner using, as his excuse, that earlier at Aquascogoc the Savages had stolen a silver cup belonging to Sir Grenville. Menatonon's and Skiko's hands were tied behind them and the three remaining warriors chased back into the woodlands. Reis thought it was not a good thing to capture this crippled chief. Surely it would only antagonize the Savages. But he kept his thoughts to himself as Lane and Menatonon engaged in heated discussion for two days following, while Hariot translated all.

By the end of the second night, Menatonon had revealed that the Mangoaks had great quantities of copper, "beautifying their houses with great plenty of the same," Hariot translated. Menatonon called the mineral "Wassador" and told Ralph Lane it was plentiful in Chaunis Temoaton to the west. Or if he preferred, there was a great deep-water harbor to the north and a chief of those tribes who had pearls in great quantity. Because of this good news, Master Lane authorized Beale to put aside his musket and untie the chief, who limped away into the woods there to be surrounded by his three followers who had waited patiently for him. But Lane kept Skiko prisoner.

Unfamiliar with the politics of it all, Reis kept away from where they were discussing, busying himself with helping Joachim and Altschmer with the furnace. He brought more food to Jeremie and told him to wait to return to camp.

"At least until Master Lane is finished with the Savage."

By now Jeremie had developed a deep cough which he tried to muffle in his jacket as best he could. Reis was sorely worried that the boy would get sicker if he didn't get closer to the fire. He decided to ask Joachim that evening.

Joachim said not a word when Reis told him about Jeremie but his eyebrows furrowed deeper when Reis mentioned Jeremie's cough.

"Bring him here," said Joachim Gans and Reis nodded. He knew that if Jeremie got even more sick and died, that it would be his fault for hiding him and not telling anyone. When he saw that Jeremie couldn't walk he ran back and got his master.

"He can't get up," Reis cried out and followed Joachim to where Jeremie lay, still hidden deep in the brambles. Joachim grunted as the thorns tore at his clothing but he managed to drag Jeremie out and lifted him in his arms to take him back to camp.

No one saw them go to Joachim's shelter, for Lane, Amadas, Hariot and the others were conferring about Menatonon's news. Joachim laid Jeremie on his blanket and began rubbing his hands and feet.

"He is half-frozen, boy," said Joachim with a voice as cold as the frosted air.

"Be you addled in the head to let him follow us for weeks like this, without warmth and proper food?"

Jeremie coughed and moaned. Reis was stricken with guilt, for even in the half-light of the tent he could see how pale was Jeremie's skin and how frail he looked. He knelt down by Jeremie's side.

"How be you feeling now?"

Jeremie whispered,

"My chest hurts when I breathe."

Joachim rose and gave Reis a push.

"Bid Master Altschmer to heat some water to boiling. Tell Master Hariot I must speak with him."

Reis ran to do what he was told. Master Altschmer pumped the bellows against the flames and the fire roared hot. He put a black kettle on to boil and fanned the flames some more.

When Sir Thomas heard Reis's news he left the group and went immediately to Joachim's tent.

"How bad is he?" Sir Thomas asked.

"Bad enough," answered Joachim, giving Reis a stern look. Reis hung his head. Why, oh why had he not told Joachim sooner? He berated himself over and over until Master Hariot took pity on him and bade him leave. Reis went back to where Master Altschmer was and took over the heavy bellows until the water boiled merrily. The smelter himself carried the hot kettle over to Joachim's tent where he placed it on the earth near Jeremie. They brought a cloth and covered Jeremie's head and the kettle's vapors, so that the steam could rise and break his congestion. Joachim mixed a paste of leaves and herbs and rubbed the sticky mixture onto Jeremie's chest. He coughed incessantly.

Reis spent a restless night listening to Jeremie and the low murmurs of Hariot and Lane, who had come to watch. A strange heartache was welling inside his chest and he knew for certain its source, guilt and fear and a foreboding of bad things to come. He tossed and moaned in his sleep, waking frequently to cock his head and listen to the sounds of the night, the hooting of the owls, the distant howling of wolves, the rasping cough of his young friend.

CHAPTER 14
THE PLANS OF PEMISAPAN

THE NEWS OF Pemisapan's hostility greatly disturbed Ralph Lane and the others. They met the next morn to discuss strategies. It seemed that Ensenore had died. Ensenore, who had been the father of Pemisapan and a member of his council, believed that the English held special powers and had urged caution in dealing with them. Now that he was dead, Pemisapan was planning a massive attack jointly with Tarraquine and Andacon, chiefs of the neighboring tribes. Skiko, who did not appear a reluctant prisoner, had revealed all of this to Philip Amadas.

"My father wishes to keep the peace. He is meeting with his warriors and will return soon."

Reis walked over to where Jeremie lay. The boy had spent a restless night, coughing harshly and sometimes moaning aloud. Several times the kettle had been re-boiled and Jeremie made to breathe its vapors. Master Gans had added special herbs to the boiling water, their fumes stinging the eyes of Hariot and himself. But they stayed by Jeremie's side all through the night. At dawn's light Reis had stumbled out of bed and made his way to his master's tent, intending to ask about his friend. But he was met by Sir Thomas as he was just leaving.

"Hist boy, let him sleep. 'Tis the first time he's slept without coughing. Leave him be."

"Will he be all right?"

Sir Thomas hesitated.

"He's still poorly. Joachim tells me that you knew of his following us and said not a word. Why is that?"

Reis was so distraught he could hardly speak.

"He... made me promise... not to tell. He was afraid...."

"Afraid of what?"

"That Sir Ralph would send him back to the main camp. Especially after being told he couldn't come with us."

Master Hariot frowned.

"Your oath of silence may have cost his life."

"Master Hariot, what can I do?"

The great astronomer and mathematician walked past him.

"Say your prayers, boy, and hope that Almighty God is listening. For we've much need of prayers now, for the boy and with Pemisapan's anger on the rise."

Reis started after him, wishing he could be just like him and knowing he probably never would. Now even Joachim Gans was thinking badly of him for not telling anyone about Jeremie and because of it, the boy was ill and maybe dying. Reis did his tasks with his mind numb and his eyes glazed with worry. He wondered if he should take Master Hariot's advice and pray to God.

But talking to the Almighty was not an easy thing. Reis

wasn't used to praying and though he tried to remember the psalms that Uncle Allyn had taught him or even the Our Father, he got no further than three lines of each before his mind ran dry. For the fourth time that day he wandered close to the tent of his master and listened to Jeremie's deeply congested cough.

"Hist now," said Master Altschmer's deep voice in his ear. "You can not do gut by vaiting around like this. Come here und help mit this fire."

Master Altschmer beckoned him to follow and Reis did, the guilt like a stone in his stomach. Though he hadn't eaten much all day, he felt the bile rise and he retched by a clump of bushes, again and again until his stomach cramped and his eyes ran tears. If Master Altschmer heard he said nothing but waited by the furnace until Reis joined him.

There was something about the German smelter that Reis liked, even though he was Master Greutter's friend. He was a big solid man with arms like tree trunks and a neck just as thick. His face was always red from the fire's heat and beads of sweat ran continuously down his face dripping into his beard, which he wiped away with a large blue kerchief.

"Vork ist the best thing," he said after a few minutes. Reis was pumping the bellows, opening and closing them so the air was driven onto the flames. With each puff the fire sparked and burned hotter. Reis felt his skin grow flush and he could smell the metallic odor of the roasting ores.

"You pump the bellows gut, boy," chuckled the smelter. "The fire vants to go to sleep but you vill not let it. Gut, gut! Vielleicht werden Sie ein Schmelzer sein."

Reis felt the ache in his shoulders but he kept the bellows

opening and closing. The heat was almost unbearable, so close was he to the flames. Open and close, open and close, his arms moved almost like the beating of his heart. He must have worked the bellows for a long time without realizing it for when the smelter took them from his iron grip, his arms still pumped in a rhythmic beat.

"Hist, mein little one," said Master Altschmer in a strange, soft voice. "You must stop und rest."

Reis shook his head stubbornly and reached for the bellows again. Master Altschmer laid them on the side of the stonework and studied Reis with a careful eye.

"You are ill?"

Reis shook his head again. The German looked as if he were going to say something else, then changed his mind. He tested the liquid ore, scooping some off in an iron ladle and tipping the ladle this way and that to see how the melt ran. Not satisfied, he poured it back into the mixture still above the fire.

"Ah, patience," he said slowly. "One must haf the patience." He stared again at Reis. "Your master, Joachim Gans, he ist a patient man. Alvays for him the time moves slowly."

Reis nodded, content now to sit and watch Altschmer at work. For this man knew what he was doing, that was certain. He never ran the fire to extreme so that all that was left of the burning was blackened slag. He knew when to remove the melt, that precise moment when the ore flowed to its proper consistency. He could skim the regulus off as easily as one might skim fat from boiling water. Reis knew, watching Altschmer at work, that he was seeing a true master of his craft just like Joachim.

When it was late evening, Joachim called to him from the edge of the fire's light. He glanced back at the smelter, still purging and refining the metal. Master Altschmer nodded slightly.

"Go now und see how the boy ist doing. For ve haf enough troubles vorrying about the Savages."

Reis wondered if the man could read the future as well as he read the liquid ore. He went reluctantly to his own master and watched for a sign from Joachim's eyes.

"He sleeps," said Master Gans, not quite so sternly this time. "And he is not coughing so much. We should know by tomorrow." He stared at Reis and shook his head.

"*If one man says to thee, 'Thou art a donkey,' pay no heed. If two speak thus, purchase a saddle.'* Know this boy, you have been braying loud and clear."

Reis knew it was going to be a long night. He said to Joachim, "I'd like to sleep in the tent."

Joachim thought for a moment, then nodded.

"A good thing, perhaps."

It was the longest night Reis had ever spent, except for the time after his father's death. When he had run away into the forest he'd given no thought to food, shelter or the wild creatures which roamed its dark depths. The first night he had spent high in a tree, wide awake and listening to the animal cries. Every creature had its own special sound and some were howls of hunger. Fierce wolves roamed the woodlands and even bear, he'd heard. He lay all night against the hard tree limb, trembling not only from cold but from fear. For six nights he'd hardly slept at all until his uncle came to fetch him. But strange as it was, he felt free in the forest. During the day he walked its leafy glades searching the bushes for any berries the birds had overlooked, cracking a nut with his teeth that had been left lying on the earthy floor. He watched the animals at work, the furry squirrels gathering for the winter, the raccoons washing their food in the stream, even the shuffling black bear with its cubs behind it. At those moments he quickly climbed the nearest tree and, from his safe vantage point, saw the youngsters rough-housing with each other. Deer were plentiful and rabbits, but he couldn't catch any of the swift hopping creatures.

Night was a different story, however, a dark forbidding world of danger. He lay awake most of the time listening to the hoot of the owl as it swept down on silent wings to catch some poor creature. He heard the wolves howling their loneliness and his own loneliness made him want to join in, but he didn't for fear of drawing them closer. He knew when their howls changed to an expectant baying as they loped after prey and he heard often the shrill shriek of a dying deer echoing through the darkness. At night, demons and goblins roamed the thickets having their sport of magic and evil doings. Witches hid deep in the forest, casting wicked spells.

"We know you are here," they whispered on the wind. *"We will come for you, just wait and see."*

He oft times thought he could see their yellow demon eyes staring out at him and hear them clattering the bones of their victims, just to scare him out of his wits. Hugging the tree branch, shivering in the cold, he thought, 'If I be invisible, they can not find me.' Fear of dying in the woods lost and alone, fear of starving or being found by the black forces of Satan, drove him down from his tree home when his uncle called, into the house of his taciturn uncle and sharp-tongued aunt.

It was a different kind of fear now, not of wild animals nor witches, nor even the Savages, but fear that Jeremie would, indeed, die and he was responsible. Such a burden lay heavy upon his shoulders. He struggled valiantly to stay awake, for in wakefulness Death wouldn't come and steal his friend. He knew all about Death, that black-cloaked villain who crept up to people's huts in the middle of the night and stole loved ones away. Death rubbed thin hands together and spirited away the sick, the weak, the starving, the babes born too soon and those not strong enough. Death was the specter people had learned to live with because they couldn't do anything about Him. Death would claim them all in His own good time!

He was awakened not by the dawn's light, but by hands shaking him roughly.

"Wake up, quickly now. We have visitors!"

Joachim was already dressed and walking outside the tent. Reis glanced at Jeremie who was sleeping. It seemed that his breathing was easier. But he had no time to think, for Joachim was signaling him. Together they walked toward the others and Reis saw that Menatonon had returned. It was still dark and the only light came from the fire's flames.

"Pemisapan has gathered his warriors to attack."

Reis felt a chill run up his spine. He had heard about the savagery of Wingina. It mattered not that he had changed his name, he was still given to wild swings of mood, one moment friendly, the next raging against the English intruders. Was this the start of war?

"Where is he?" Ralph Lane asked and Menatonon spoke rapidly. Sir Thomas hesitated.

"What's the matter?" Lane asked.

"He will not say more until you release his son."

Lane frowned. He signaled to Valentine Beale and the young man pointed his harquebuser directly at Menatonon.

"No, no," said Hariot urgently. "That isn't a wise move. Free Skiko and he'll tell you all."

Reluctantly Master Lane ordered Skiko's release. The son of Menatonon stepped to his side. Menatonon muttered softly.

"The English are men of their word," Hariot translated.

Menatonon went on to tell where Pemisapan was located and how many warriors were gathering. Then he turned to go.

"Wait," called Sir Thomas and handed him some beads and dolls. The crippled chief nodded his head. He and his men disappeared into the trees. Reis breathed a sigh of relief; he'd unknowingly held his breath the whole time.

"Vat happens now?" Master Haring asked. The others had joined them.

"Menatonon goes to meet with the chiefs. He will try to dissuade them from joining Pemisapan."

Ralph Lane snapped an order.

"Pack up the camp," he said. "We must be ready to move by dawn."

CHAPTER 15
THE SPONGE, THE FUNNEL,
THE SIFTER, THE SIEVE

IN THE LIGHT from the burning storehouses, Reis saw the Savages running back and forth, yelling wildly at each other. The acrid smoke billowed and curled toward the dark sky. He and the two others slipped silently away…."This will be devastation to them; all their stores for the winter have been destroyed."

"You fool, you bloody fool! If they have no food, they'll have even more provocation to attack us."

"You said to strike them where it hurts."

Ralph Lane threw up his hands in disgust. Captain Vaughan, Valentine Beale and Reis had crept upon the sleeping tribe of Pemisapan and set fire to their storehouses. It had been an action hinted at by Master Lane, though he'd not given a direct order. Now back at the camp Reis watched Lane rant and rave, watched Sir Thomas's face with its grave concern, felt Joachim's reproving stare boring holes in his back.

It was true that around the camp fire the previous night, Lane had stated that he wished to strike a blow at Pemisapan's heart. Upon hearing that Captain Vaughan had summoned

Beale and awakened Reis who, groggy with sleep, had run reluctantly with them through the woodlands several miles to the hills overlooking the great chief's encampment. Once there they had inched their way down to the storehouses and with Beale and Reis waiting, Vaughan killed the man guarding the stores and had made Reis wriggle through the opening with his lighted wick. The flames which roared forth turned blackest night into red and gold. In the confusion, the three were able to get safely away and return to Master Lane.

"Pemisapan will go on the warpath for certain," exclaimed Sir Ralph, his face carved deep with anger.

"Not so," said the captain. "He has no way of knowing it was us."

"This was not a wise decision," Master Hariot frowned. He strode back and forth shaking his head. Reis knew he was a man of peace, eager to calm any quarrels that the men might have with each other and to be their spokesman with the Savages.

Joachim called. He was gathering his belongings.

"Come help me here, for if we must move with haste, then everything should be packed away."

"Do you think Pemisapan will attack us?" Reis asked, still out of breath from the run back.

Joachim stared coldly at him.

"*Doubt cannot override a certainty.* You have much to learn, boy. Because of this foolishness, anything is possible. If he suspects us, then most assuredly. If not, then he will wait and see who claims the strike against him."

"He has enemies," Master Amadas said, walking over. "Perhaps he will blame others."

"A rash move," Joachim said sternly, still glaring at Reis. "It puts us at the disadvantage."

Master Amadas nodded, noting that the Jew made good sense.

"But perchance a lesson has been given and one learned. First he offers us food, then he cuts our weirs and we lose our fish."

They had discovered the weirs cut to shreds one late afternoon. When they first set up the main encampment upon disembarking from The Tyger, the Savages had come as friends and taught them how to make the nets and place them strategically in the river. Reis liked the weirs for it meant he didn't have to lean far out over the rushing water. But one late afternoon they had found them cut to pieces. There had been other things, too, which led them to believe the Indians were growing increasingly hostile. Pemisapan, still called Wingina at the time, had gradually withdrawn his offers of food for the coming winter months. While his brother, Granganimeo, lived there had been a muted friendship with the tribe who taught them how to plant crops and make the weirs. It was after Granganimeo died that Wingina took the name of Pemisapan, "wary and watchful," and turned his face away from the English.

Sir Thomas, always trying to see both sides, told Ralph Lane that Pemisapan's people were, perhaps, growing low on their own food reserves. He called for a meeting with the Great Chief but was met instead by Ensenore, the former manamatowick, or king, who urged caution on both sides. For a while Pemisapan appeared to be friendly again. Now all that had changed.

They backtracked at least ten miles from their last camp. Behind them lay the storehouses of Pemisapan, blackened and burned to ashes. The Savages would go looking for the attackers; their revenge would be swift and terrible.

"We left signs of the Weapemeoc," Vaughan said with bravado. "Pemisapan will think it was them and turn away from us."

Ralph Lane was furious still. He ordered Vaughan and Beale held under guard, relieving Beale of his musket. Reis was summoned before him.

"For your youth, I can not fault you. But you lack common sense and judgment. Altschmer and Master Gans are your taskmasters now."

For the next few days both men took Sir Ralph's words to heart. From dawn to dusk Reis toiled either at the furnace or by Joachim's side, digging, fetching wood, pumping the bellows, splitting kindling, scrubbing the implements, only to do those very same tasks the next day. His hands quickly blistered. As he worked, so Jeremie gained strength until one day the boy joined him in gathering sticks.

"It's good to see you," Reis remarked, feeling the truth of his words. Though his cough lingered, Jeremie seemed well enough. He was thinner than Reis remembered and his skin without color. Reis made sure to carry the heavier branches, leaving the twigs for Jeremie.

"'Tis good to see you, too. I thought perhaps I might die."

"We thought so," Reis agreed then seeing Jeremie's face, added, "but Joachim said you would not."

"They say Joachim has magic in his herbs, that he cast a spell upon me to chase away the evil spirits."

Reis paused, giving Jeremie's words careful thought. Then he shook his head. The boy's illness was simply the ague; there had been no magic involved in his cure. But he needed more time to reflect. Life was, indeed, a topsy-turvy experience; one moment basking in his master's praise, the next feeling the coldness of Joachim's dark, brooding eyes upon him. He thought it unfair to be punished for what Captain Vaughan had done, wakening him in the middle of the night and prodding him through the deep forest toward Pemisapan's camp. Why should he be punished for obeying orders? Now he was living daily under Joachim's reproachful gaze. Reis thought that his lot in life hadn't changed much from the days with his uncle.

Joachim called him over after chores that evening. He walked to his master's tent, wondering what chastisement would be his. Had he not cleaned the boots properly? Or perhaps he'd not gathered enough wood to bank the fire. Lately he much preferred the scathing sarcasm of Master Greutter, or the quick temper of Ralph Lane, to Joachim's cold, deliberate words.

"You feel you have been unjustly punished?"

Reis took in a deep breath. How could his master know exactly what he was thinking? Joachim was studying him carefully.

"You puzzle how I know, so I will tell you. Your face is plain for all to read, anger, resentment that you should be held accountable for the actions of others. Even that you were only following Vaughan's orders." He paused. "Master Lane is for sending you back to the main camp with Jeremie, Vaughan and Beale."

Reis's mouth dropped open. It was the thing he feared most.

"Look not at the bottle, but what it contains."

Reis frowned. He had no idea what his master meant by those strange words. Amazingly, Joachim gave one of his rare smiles.

"It is from the Talmud. Know you what it means?"

He shook his head.

"Of course you do. Think carefully."

Again Reis shook his head. His master was playing games with him as a cat might do with a mouse.

"No," said Joachim as if reading his thoughts. "'Tis not a game. Have you no idea?"

Reis was silent. It was unnerving to have Joachim probing his mind. The Jew sighed deeply.

"Then I will tell you. I see before me not just a young foolish apprentice, but the man he may become. The others, perhaps, see only the container. Do you understand?"

Reis wasn't sure. Why did Joachim speak so in riddles? He stared back at his master who saw the puzzlement still in his eyes.

"I will not tell you any more. Go now and think about what I've said."

"Master Gans," Reis began, then hesitated. But his master had already closed the opening to his tent and he was left to walk in silence back to where he slept.

Reis wasn't good at riddles. Quick-minded though he was, they perplexed him. "What is bright like a penny, yet hides behind a veil of tears?" His cousins had taunted him for all the days he'd tried to figure it out. "Why, 'tis the sun, you addle-brained dolt." And he finally understood; the sun shone brightly in the heavens then hid when the rain clouds came.

He wanted to shout that he knew it all along and was just teasing them like they teased him. But he said not a word while they laughed and thumbed their noses, until his aunt came from the house scolding and slapping in all directions.

One time in the early days of their sojourn north, Joachim had told him of the four kinds of students who wanted to learn the Talmud.

"The first is like a sponge. He absorbs all and digests little, regurgitating it upon command. The second is a funnel, for everything that goes in simply pours right out. The third is a sifter for he remembers only the trivial and forgets the important. The last is a sieve for he works through everything, weighing the significance and relative worth of each argument. He puts great effort into his understanding. He is the most focused of all."

Then Joachim had looked with curiosity at him.

"Which one are you?"

Indeed Reis thought now, I still don't know which I am. He had thought perhaps he could be the sponge, soaking everything up, filling all the spaces of his mind. Then he thought he might surely burst with so much accumulated knowledge and not even Joachim knew everything, so how could HE ever hope to? Maybe his master thought him the funnel, with some knowledge flowing in then pouring out just as quickly. Worse yet, he could be the sifter, remembering trivialities and forgetting what was important. If he were the sieve, 'twould be wondrous indeed, yet he knew not what was important enough to retain and what was incidental. It was a real puzzlement and he dwelt on it for many days after his master told him the story. Which student am I? he pondered over and over. Which one does Joachim wish me to be? How will I ever know? How will I ever measure up?

He found it difficult to sleep that night. Sometimes he heard moaning and awoke startled, thinking it was Jeremie. But the boy slept dreamlessly, except for an occasional cough. Perhaps the moaning was the wind in the bare branches, causing them to crack against each other and echo with a hollow sound. Could the moaning have been some animal wandering close to the camp, ravenous yet afraid to approach and steal the scraps? He awoke in the grey mist of dawn, a dampness upon his face that was neither sweat nor rain. He awoke to muffled sounds, a pall of anguish, fear hanging like a low-lying cloud, and a knife in the hand of Pemisapan's warrior cold against the skin of his neck.

CHAPTER 16
CAPTURED

THEY WERE ROUNDED up like sheep, dull-witted with the cobwebs of sleep still clinging to them. Master Haring was nursing a wound on his arm and Ralph Lane bled from the scalp. Jeremie was crumpled on the ground and there he lay. Reis wondered if he were dead. He looked for Joachim and saw him sitting on a tree stump with a Savage watching him. The bow was at the ready with a drawn arrow pointed right at his heart.

Masters Greutter and Altschmer were muttering low in their German tongue until a blow from the hand of Pemisapan silenced them both. The leader of the Savages was an imposing figure, tall for an Indian with jet-black hair pulled back in a tail and feathers intertwined. He nodded his head and Thomas Hariot was brought before him. Pemisapan spoke in a low voice and at great length. The anger in him was evident in his stance and the boldness of his look. Sir Thomas answered him in the same language and Reis could understand neither.

Then Ralph Lane was forced forward. Pemisapan took his knife and held it at Lane's throat. Reis saw that Master Lane hid his fear well; Reis's own legs were trembling and his bowels were like water. Ralph Lane said something and Hariot translated, yet Pemisapan clearly was not pleased. He gave a nod of his head and two warriors prodded Valentine Beale forward. The young harquebusier licked his lips in fear and tried not to show his terror. Sir Thomas quickly said something and stepped in front of the warriors. Pemisapan muttered an answer, pushed Hariot roughly aside and with one swift movement, cut the throat of Valentine Beale. The young soldier tried to talk, gurgled something as the blood rushed out, then rolled his eyes back and slumped to the ground, blood still pumping from his wound.

"Here now!" Ralph Lane called out in alarm but Pemisapan paid no attention. Without hesitation he walked to where Captain Vaughan was standing and, in the same swift movement, slashed open his throat. The captain fell to the ground drowning in his own blood. A musket shot rang out, missing its target. One of Pemisapan's warriors loosed an arrow and the other harquebusier fell to the ground, the shaft protruding from his chest. Reis's heart was pounding in fear. Surely the Savages would hear! Pemisapan walked to where he was standing. Reis could see the blood staining his knife blade. He gulped and tried to swallow but almost choked. The chief looked down on him and Reis died a thousand deaths. He closed his eyes and waited for the sharp pain of the knife drawn across his throat. He staggered and almost fell, feeling Joachim's arm holding him up. When he opened his eyes Pemisapan had turned away.

They were pushed and prodded forward leaving the bodies of Beale, Vaughan and the other where they had fallen, without even benefit of a Christian burial. Master Haring half-carried, half-led Jeremie, who had barely recovered from his faint. Thomas Hariot was talking with Pemisapan, who appeared not to answer yet did nothing to stop him. They were forced to a trot, then a run, miles and miles through the still-misted forest toward their enemy's camp. Above the grunts of the Savages and the thud of their feet, Reis heard Jeremie's labored breathing.

They were herded together into an enclosure, closely guarded by Savages with painted faces. Jeremie had begun to cough again, loud racking spasms from the forced run and the dampness. Joachim moved closer to him, keeping Reis by his side. The warriors watched them with stone black eyes.

And so they waited, kept in that compound for three days and nights. No water or food was provided. Jeremie coughed and coughed; Reis's stomach growled its hunger pangs, yet not a Savage came with sustenance. At one point Sir Thomas was taken from them and marched toward Pemisapan's tent.

"Ve vill not see him again," muttered Greutter. "He ist done for."

"Be silent," warned Philip Amadas. "Do nothing to anger them further."

"They are already angry," retorted Master Greutter. He turned belligerently to face Joachim.

"Vat say you, Master Gans, do you haf a potion up your sleeve for this?"

"Aber nein," said Altschmer, pulling his friend away. "No fighting among us. Wir müssen nicht mit einander kämpfen."

Joachim shook his head.

"I have no magic," he said. "Only reason."

Greutter snorted contemptuously.

"Reason vill not help us here. Ve need muskets, mein heathen freund, that ist vat ve need."

"We are outnumbered, mein freund," replied Joachim, nodding at the guards who surrounded them. "We were twelve, now nine, plus two boys. Master Hariot is our hope."

"He hast betrayed us," Greutter's voice rose. "He hast made a deal mit the enemy to save himself. You vill see, Gans, you vill see I am right."

When Hariot did not return even Reis wondered if what Greutter had said was true. The fourth day came and went. At dusk, water and food was brought but it was barely enough to wet their lips and ease the hunger pains.

By now Jeremie had developed a fever. His skin was flushed and he trembled. Spasms seized his chest.

"He was but barely recovering when we left camp," whispered Joachim, ministering to him. "The run and the cold have done him in."

"Will he die?"

"Perhaps, if we do not get him into warmth."

"Then I shall try," said Reis, though he felt himself trembling at the prospect of what he was about to do.

"Try what?" asked Joachim, staring at his apprentice.

Reis got up from the ground by Jeremie's side and walked over to one of the Savages. The warrior watched him curiously, his face betraying neither surprise nor anger.

"My friend is sick," Reis said in a timorous voice. He knew the Indians would not understand his English words but perhaps they might respond to his gestures. He pointed to Jeremie, pretended to cough, then feigned falling to the ground. When he picked himself up he saw the Savage had not moved except to draw his long knife and hold it before him.

"He is sick," Reis said again, then watched in horror as the Savage pantomimed slitting his throat. He backed hurriedly away and returned to Joachim's side.

"Not a good move," his master whispered. "Do not stray from me again."

Reis wondered what manner of men these Savages were, not to offer help to a boy so sick as Jeremie. He heard Joachim muttering something under his breath. It was in Hebrew.

"Master?" he tugged on the Jew's arm. "Are you praying to your God?"

"Yours, mine, one and the same. *A good deed leads to another, but one evil deed brings disaster in its wake.*"

"What is that?"

Reis couldn't fathom the mind of Joachim Gans. Why was he spouting words from the Talmud again? How could that help them now?

"If Hariot does not return soon, then I will go and speak to this chief."

"See, see!" cried Master Greutter, his voice rising in panic. "He comes und Hariot ist not mit him!"

The great chief strode to the compound. He said something to one of the warriors. The Savage unlocked the opening and walked toward Joachim Gans. He motioned for him to follow.

"Vork your magic now, Master Gans," whispered Greutter, his voice breaking. "Speak und persuade them to let us go."

Joachim shook his head.

"I know not their language."

He stood his ground. Angrily, the Indian began to push him. Once again, Joachim shook his head. He pointed to Jeremie lying on the ground. Pemisapan grunted and the Savage stepped back, allowing Joachim to pick Jeremie up and carry him in his arms.

Joachim was gone a long time. Reis shivered both from cold and a terrible fear. If the Savages had already killed Master Hariot, what would be Joachim's fate? He had heard tales of these natives plucking out the hearts of their victims and eating the still-beating organ. Perhaps they had already done so with Sir Thomas and even now, were holding poor Jeremie's heart in their bloody hands. He trembled as if with the ague; not even Master Altschmer's jacket thrown about his shoulders could stave off the tremors.

Not a sign of Master Hariot or Joachim Gans appeared. The cold night passed slowly. Reis heard his own teeth chattering inside his head like a reverberating drum. He pulled Altschmer's jacket around him and over his head, grateful for the kindness of the smelter who sat with his back against Greutter's for warmth. Reis shuddered when he thought about Valentine Beale. The young soldier had been kind, telling him many stories about his life back in England and how he had been conscripted into service. He was, perhaps, only nineteen or so, not that many years older than Reis. And Captain Vaughan had always been a good man, though impulsive. It was his rash behavior which had brought about their downfall. Joachim had known what might happen if the Savages discovered who had burned their storehouse. Joachim always knew what the future might bring. Oh, where was his master now? What fate had befallen him in Pemisapan's tent?

The sun was rising on the fifth morn when Sir Thomas appeared out of the mist and walked toward their compound. For all this time the men and women of Pemisapan's tribe had watched them, chattering excitedly in their own strange tongue, poking at them with sticks. Some of the young children had hurled stones their way. Master Altschmer and Philip Amadas had been hit with the flying rocks. Reis stared at these boys and girls, some younger than he, others the same age. They had bronze skin and jet black hair. The boys tried to impress their elders by parading up and down in the manner of warriors. If Reis hadn't been the prisoner, he might have found their posturing amusing. But in their childish arrogance, they frightened him.

Thomas Hariot looked gaunt and troubled. His demeanor was cautious. He approached the compound and signaled one of the warriors. The man grudgingly allowed him to pass and enter. Hariot went immediately to Sir Ralph and Amadas, where they conferred in whispers. Reis moved closer to Altschmer. Now that Joachim had gone, he felt alone and the presence of the big German smelter gave him some comfort. Altschmer smiled at him while Greutter eyed him warily.

"Perhaps you know the magic, eh?" he whispered hoarsely. "He hast taught you the spells, hast he not? You know vat to do."

"Leave the boy, Erhart," said Master Altschmer.

"Nein, nein, he knows. The Jew hast taught him. Come here, boy."

Reis walked reluctantly to the miner.

"Can you vork magic?"

Reis shook his head. Greutter frowned. He pulled Reis closer.

"Gans hast taught you. You can set us free. Ve need you, boy. Your master hast deserted us und gone to the enemy's side. Vy ist he not here mit us?"

Reis tried to pull away but Greutter held him tightly. He began to push and struggled against the miner's grip until, finally, it was Altschmer who grabbed his friend's hands and broke them free. He spoke in rapid German and Reis moved quickly away, positioning himself closer to Sir Thomas and Master Lane. Sir Thomas came over and knelt down in front of him.

"Your friend is dead," he said with great sorrow. "Nothing we did could save the boy."

CHAPTER 17
POWER PLAY

REIS DIDN'T KNOW how he got through the rest of that terrible time. Upon hearing Master Hariot's news, he stared straight ahead. There were no tears that forced their way through his eyelids. He wouldn't let these Savages nor, indeed, anyone see him weep for Jeremie. What was the boy to him, after all? Not a close friend of the heart, a mere apprentice like himself, sold to the highest bidder. Jeremie had called Joachim the Christ killer. He had denounced his master for drinking the blood of Christian babes. Surely one so full of ignorance wouldn't be missed at all? Then why did he feel so terrible? Why did his heart grieve so? He stared stonily into space, neither seeing nor hearing those around him.

One young Savage, no more than eight, slipped into the compound and squatted down in front of Reis. He was thin and his ribs showed through his skin. He cocked his head to one side. Reis saw the burning of his eyes and the gaze unnerved him. He got up and moved closer to the others. The boy followed. Reis noticed the guarding warriors did nothing. When he moved a third time, the boy followed once more.

"What do you want?" Reis asked, though he knew the boy couldn't understand. The young Indian held out his hand. It was empty. 'What does he want?' It was a puzzlement. 'I have nothing at all,' he thought. Then he reached into the jacket pocket and felt a lump of metal. He drew it out to stare at the iron ore. The boy grunted. Reis rolled the small nugget around in his fingers. It was worthless, just a piece from the slag heap. Again the boy grunted and without a word, Reis handed it to him. The boy whooped in triumph, stood up and ran past the guard to the other children who had watched. They crowded around him.

"They can trade it," Master Hariot said, coming over. "It will buy them some food."

"It's worthless," said Reis and those were the first words he'd spoken since hearing about Jeremie. "Why would they want a useless piece of ore?"

"They have no real monies, just what they can barter for. They're as hungry as we. The burning of their storehouse was the final blow. Some of them want to kill us all."

Reis shuddered.

"Where is my master?"

"They hold him in Pemisapan's tent. He is different from us, as well you know. They think him magic."

So Master Greutter had hit upon the truth after all. Even the Savages thought Joachim Gans was a spell-caster.

"Will they harm him?"

"Not as long as we are still talking. When Pemisapan shuts his ears to our words, who knows what may happen."

Reis rummaged around in the jacket's other pocket. He found nothing. He thought about the boy who had snatched the piece of useless ore in triumph. What could he trade it for? How much food was it worth? Perhaps they could use that to their advantage. He got up and sat down next to Master Haring. The man's face was grim.

"Master Haring," he whispered. "Have you any metal?"

Master Haring stared at him.

"Vat are you talking about?"

"They want metal. They can trade it with other tribes for food. Do you have anything?"

Over to the side, Greutter threw back his head and gave a chuckle.

"All vas left at the camp," he said. "There ist plenty of metal there. Tell them that, boy."

At the sound of Greutter's loud voice, the warriors on guard stiffened. He stared at them and they stared back. Reis went to each of the men. Philip Amadas took out the flints he carried and looked at them.

"Perhaps we can use these," he said.

Master Lane dismissed him with a wave of his hand.

"There's no metal here. Don't be ridiculous, boy. Sit you down and be still before you anger them further."

Master Hariot went back to Pemisapan's tent. He was gone until the next morn. By that time Reis was beginning to cough himself and the other men were clearly showing signs of the cold. The Savages had wrapped cloaks around themselves made of the thick fur of animals. A few skins were thrown into the compound and the men covered themselves in these. Reis was glad Master Altschmer had one, for he had taken the jacket back from the smelter to huddle in its warmth. The day passed slowly and within the confines of his prison Reis walked, scuffing his feet and kicking small stones to entertain himself. At one point Master Altschmer joined him.

"You are scared?"

Reis nodded, not trusting himself to speak.

"Me, too."

He stopped and looked at the big man walking next to him.

"Ist true. Greutter und me, Haring, all scared but not to show it in front of them. Es ist besser, Angst nicht zu zeigen."

"Do you think they'll kill us?"

Altschmer paused.

"They do not think like us. They are angry. Ve are guilty. Punishment ist due."

"But... but...."

"Nein, nein, do not vorry, ist not you they vant."

He stopped and looked up at the sky.

"Snow soon," he said. "Back home it vud start the Holy time."

Unexpectedly he reached out and ruffled Reis's hair.

"Master Hariot speaks for us. Und your master, too, Joachim ist... he ist...."

"... a good man."

Altschmer nodded.

"Ja, if he hast magic, like Erhart says, ve haf much need of it now."

The Indians watched and said nothing. Late in the afternoon one of the warriors strode into the compound and grabbed Reis roughly by the arm. He tried to resist but it was no use. The Indian propelled him forcefully toward the great chief's tent. Behind him he heard the angry roar of Master

Gruetter, who had risen threateningly when the Savage first entered. Greutter began swinging his fists and it took three warriors to subdue him and push him forward. He and Reis found themselves thrust inside to face Pemisapan.

Reis gasped. At least it was warm. There was a small fire burning in the center, the smoke wafting out the hole at the top. Joachim was there and still alive. Reis was never so glad to see anyone in his life. Master Hariot gave him a slight nod then signaled him to sit and be quiet. To Greuttter, he did the same.

"Vat ist this?" the big miner growled. He glared at Joachim and took a threatening step toward him, fists raised.

"Jew bastard, you hast taken their side!"

Master Hariot half-rose, Joachim sat with his head bowed. Greutter advanced more threateningly toward him, ignoring Pemisapan standing there watching his every move. The chief muttered something in his strange language. Hariot quickly translated. Joachim spoke and Hariot translated for Pemisapan.

"Tell him I can not."

The chief spoke again but this time, Hariot remained silent while Joachim slowly shook his head.

"It is impossible for me to do so."

"Was ist los?" Greutter questioned, whirling around so fast that he bumped into the chief, almost knocking him over. Pemisapan looked at one of his warriors and the Indian strode quickly forward and with his drawn knife, slashed down at Greutter's ear. The big man gave a howl and clapped his hand where his ear had been. Reis's heart turned over. Blood was spurting everywhere, large spatters of it covering Joachim and Pemisapan. The Indian warrior quickly slipped behind Greutter and held the knife to his throat. Pemisapan said some more words and Hariot stared at him, started to open his mouth to speak, but the chief waved him silent. Greutter was moaning, trying to stop the blood from gushing where his ear had been. Joachim spoke through Hariot.

"Let him go, Great Chief."

Pemisapan shook his head. Hariot spoke Joachim's words again and once more, Pemisapan shook his head. The chief held out his hand but Joachim said and did nothing. Greutter kicked out violently toward Pemisapan and the knife point pricked his skin.

Then Joachim leaned forward and whispered quickly in Reis's ear.

"If silence be good for the wise, how much better for fools? Say nothing, do nothing, do you understand?"

Reis was too fearful even to nod. He sat like one turned to stone while Greutter howled and the warrior pulled him backward out of the tent. Two others left also and they heard Greutter's cry of protest as he was pushed deep into the woods.

"Was ist los, eh, eh...?"

Reis began to tremble violently. As the tremors shook him he felt Joachim's hand soft upon his arm. Joachim was saying something in Hebrew under his breath. Reis knew that Master Greutter was going to die. Without being told he knew it deep in his heart. Though he disliked the man intensely, he would not wish him this particular fate nor, indeed, anyone. He thought of Valentine Beale and Captain Vaughan, he thought of Jeremie's untimely death.

Against the backdrop of Greutter's cries of agony rising

and falling, echoing back in waves from the deep dark trees, Reis heard the chorus of witches, howling in delight. Only Joachim's hand on his arm kept him from jumping up to run screaming from the tent. Only Joachim's gaze fixed upon his face kept him quiet. Pemisapan was watching. Joachim's lips moved slowly; he lowered his bared head, his ear curls clearly showing. His long black coat was off and he looked like a man who has sat himself down with friends after a big meal, saying first his prayers then waiting for the right moment to engage in deep conversation.

Staring at Pemisapan's impassive face, watching Joachim Gans with his head bowed, Reis was suddenly aware of what was happening here. It was the play of power against power. Joachim held power over the Great Chief, who wanted something that his master wouldn't give. Joachim had somehow convinced Pemisapan he had strong magic, that he could render spells. Pemisapan had known all along it was the English who burned his storehouses not the Weapemeoc, in spite of Weapemeoc arrow heads left by Vaughan and Beale. Pemisapan had planned their slaughter and only Joachim, with his strange looks and even stranger ways, stood between them and certain death.

CHAPTER 18
A BARGAIN STRUCK

LONG AFTER GREUTTER'S screams had stopped and silence fallen, Reis could still hear him. Only once during that interminable time while Pemisapan sat cross-legged, fixed and immovable, Joachim had lifted his hand from Reis's arm, leaned slightly forward and mouthed the words,

"I could not stop it."

Reis shook his head. It mattered not. Greutter was dead, tortured in those dark dismal woods, his cries rising to a God whose ears were closed against him. Greutter had been a man full of hatred and prejudice, yet no one deserved to die in that manner. Had Master Gans, in some inexplicable way, singled him out? Could he have saved him? These were questions for which he had no answers. He found it hard to believe ill of his master but Joachim was acting strangely now, swaying side to side as he had done before, silently mouthing Hebrew words. Reis's dream rushed back to him, the lamb whose throat was cut, its blood pouring out, the lamb changing form. Could it really have been the Christ? Might it not be Erhart Greutter, sacrificed to assuage Pemisapan's cold anger?

At one point the chief rose and summoned Joachim and Hariot from the tent. While they were gone, Reis turned his face away and let the tears run unchecked down his cheeks. Beale, Vaughan, the other harbusquier, Jeremie and now, Greutter. Who would be next? After a while, the warrior on guard led him back to the compound. Reis wiped his eyes furiously. Master Altschmer all but knocked him down in his haste to find out what had happened.

"These screams I kept hearing, ist Greutter?"

"They took him away," Reis choked on the words. "They... they...."

Altschmer put his hands to his face. For a moment, Reis thought he was weeping. Then the big man turned and walked away. Ralph Lane was called into Pemisapan's tent. He went and Reis watched him go with a heavy heart. Was Sir Ralph to suffer the same fate as Master Greutter? And who would be next: Stafford, Amadas, Master Haring? Finally, there was Reis Courtney. Would Pemisapan have him taken into the woods, there to be tortured and cut to pieces? And what of Sir Thomas and Joachim Gans? Had Joachim, indeed, made a pact with Pemisapan? Spare my life and I will give you the others? Spare only me and you shall have your revenge?

When Pemisapan appeared it was without the three men. He walked deliberately into the compound and stared at the rest of them waiting there. His eyes swept over each one in turn. Philip Amadas held out the flints from his pocket. The chief took them and Reis thought that was a good thing. Pemisapan's eyes missed nothing, from Altschmer's downcast demeanor to Haring's sullen expression, to Stafford's anxious look. His eyes fixed on each one and came to rest on Reis.

He tried not to tremble, staring back into the chief's dark black eyes. 'Because of you,' he thought, 'Jeremie is dead and Master Greutter. Because of you....'

Pemisapan grunted and gave a signal. One of his warriors moved toward Reis and beckoned him. It was a strangely English gesture but even so, Reis's heart skipped a beat. He got up slowly, glanced back at the others, then followed Pemisapan out of the compound to the edge of the woods.

Much later Reis could only wonder at what Joachim had been trying to do. A crude assay furnace of stone had been constructed near the tree line. The fire beneath it was roaring fiercely. In front of the furnace Joachim was roasting metal nuggets in a makeshift pan. The nuggets were already liquefying under the intensity. Waves of heat rose from the flames and the acrid smell of burning filled the air.

From his pockets Joachim produced his own nuggets and dropped them into the molten ore while Pemisapan watched. Joachim let the fire build to a white-hot core. At one point he called for Master Altschmer and the big man was brought forth from the compound.

When Altschmer saw what was happening, he quickly went to Joachim's side, fanning the flames, measuring the liquid metal, testing it, scooping off the regulus. The two of them worked over the fire until their faces were red and their eyes tearing. The liquid ore was cooled, skimmed, roasted yet again, cooled, skimmed, roasted a third and fourth time until the final cooling by being plunged into pots of icy river water. At each stage of the process the metal was further refined. When at last they were finished, Pemisapan stepped forward and examined the newly-formed nuggets. His face was impassive as he rolled them in his hands, feeling their bulk, seeing their color.

Reis knew that his master was trying to show the Savages how to refine crude ore with its traces of copper into copper of the purest kind, using the same innovative process he had become famous for at the Keswick mines in England. But he had neither the right equipment nor the proper amount of time. Through his methods at Keswick, he had proved one could refine copper in only a few days instead of the twenty-two weeks it normally took. He had tried to accomplish the same thing in hours. Pemisapan's face betrayed no emotion, neither satisfaction nor anger. It was impossible to know what he was thinking as he turned and walked away from the heat of the fire, leaving them all to wonder. Master Altschmer let the great fire die down; the flames which had turned metal to liquid were allowed to subside and given no more wood to feed their insatiable hunger. Lane, Hariot and Joachim stood around with Reis at their side as the fire sank to embers, and the chill of the winter night crept closer.

The next morn Joachim shook Reis awake. The men were gathering together, wrapping their borrowed animal cloaks around them. Pemisapan was striding toward the compound, his warriors with him. As he entered the enclosure Reis couldn't stop from trembling again. The Great Chief waved his arms and spoke directly to Hariot, who translated to all.

"He congratulates the Magic One for his skill with metal." Hariot nodded in Joachim's direction. "He wishes to learn more. Therefore," and here Hariot paused.

"Well?" demanded Ralph Lane, stepping forward.

"He offers to release all of us in exchange… for the services of Master Gans, Altschmer and the young apprentice."

Reis felt Joachim's hand upon his shoulder to steady him. His legs were weak. To stay there with the Savages, surely Master Lane wouldn't allow it? He glanced over at the smelter, whose face was set in a grim smile. Joachim approached Hariot and together they conferred, talking in whispers.

"I will stay," Reis heard Joachim stay. "Maybe Altschmer, if he wants. But not the boy, he must go back with the others. Tell him that."

Sir Thomas spoke rapidly with Pemisapan. The Indian shook his head. When he'd finished speaking, Hariot turned again to them.

"He will not move on this demand. Your freedom for Joachim's skill, Altschmer and the boy as well."

Master Lane moved forward and as he did so, a dozen bows were quickly strung and pointed his way. He stopped.

"We can't leave the boy. What does he wish with him?"

Sir Thomas started to speak with Pemisapan, who silenced him with a wave of one hand. Joachim stepped forward and one warrior drew his knife. Pemisapan turned and spoke sharply in his strange dialect. The knife was sheathed.

"Tell him I will stay, Altschmer as well. The boy goes with you."

But before Sir Thomas could translate his master's words, the Savages were crowding them toward the opening in the compound, separating Altschmer, Joachim and Reis to one side, watching while their comrades left.

"Tell him," Sir Ralph called, "that I thank him for our freedom but take it with great reluctance. Tell him that no harm should come to the boy nor any of them, for if it does he will feel the true anger of the English."

As Hariot translated, Reis still couldn't believe they would actually leave him and the other two. He wanted to run after them, 'Take me, take me, don't leave me with these Savages. Look what they did to Master Greutter!' But Joachim's hand was gripping his shoulder so tightly that he couldn't move even if he dared. He watched them leave and head south toward their camp, once his but no more. His heart was filled with dread and he wondered how Joachim could remain as calm as he was.

But Joachim was already talking with the smelter, even while keeping his grip tight upon Reis's shoulder. The boy couldn't understand either one and suddenly realized that they were talking in German, something Joachim rarely did. Pemisapan watched them for a few minutes then turned and left with his men. Only one warrior remained behind and he signaled for Joachim to follow him. They were led to a small tent and pushed inside. Reis knew their every move would be watched.

When he entered the tent he gasped. For lying in one corner, covered with a cloth, was Jeremie's body. The cold had prevented decay from setting in and the Savages had brought him to this tent to await Joachim's decision. Reis went over and stared down at the young boy lying so still and white. Jeremie looked so young. His eyes were closed, yet sunken in, his skin almost translucent. Reis felt the tears stinging the backs of his eyes but he didn't cry. It was too late to weep for Jeremie. If he believed, as all Christians did, that his soul was in Heaven, then there was nothing to weep about. Joachim had already told him that the Jews, also, believed in God's Heaven and a life after death. Surely with so much belief, it was where Jeremie was right now.

"Ach, your pain ist over," muttered Altschmer, then turned to Joachim. "Vat must be done now?"

"We will ask permission to bury him."

"Ve haf no one to translate for us."

"He will understand," affirmed Joachim.

And so they buried Jeremie by the edge of the trees. Two warriors were called upon to help Joachim and Altschmer dig the deep hole. It was similar to the Indian way, who embalmed their dead in a crude fashion and buried them in the ground. Joachim had pantomimed what he wanted done and Pemisapan obliged. As soon as the hole was dug, the warriors stepped back. Joachim turned to Reis.

"Do you wish to say a prayer over your friend? It would be a good thing."

Reis nodded but couldn't think of a thing to say. He hesitated and Joachim, sensing his discomfort, stepped forward. He took off his hat and bowed his head.

"The deeper the sorrow the less tongue it hath. I will say the prayers.
Yis'ga'dal v'yis'kadash sh'may ra'bbo,
b'olmo dee'vro chir'usay v'yamlich malchu'say,
b'chayaychon uv'yomay'chon uv'chayay d'chol bais Yisroel,
ba'agolo u'viz'man koriv; v'imru Omein.
Y'hay shmay rabbo m'vorach l'olam ul'olmay olmayo.
Yisborach v'yishtabach v'yispoar v'yisromam v'yismasay,
v'yishador v'yis'aleh v'yisalal, shmay d'kudsho, brich hu,
l'aylo min kl birchoso v'sheeroso, tush'bechoso v'nechemoso,
da,ameeran b'olmo; vimru Omein.
Y'hay shlomo rabbo min sh'mayo, v'chayim alaynu v'al kol Yisroel;
v'imru Omein.

Oseh sholom bimromov, hu ya'aseh sholom olaynu, v'al kol yisroel;
vimru Omein.
May the great Name of God be exalted and sanctified, through-
out the world, which he has created according to his will. May his
Kingship be established in your lifetime and in your days, and in the
lifetime of the entire household of Israel, swiftly and in the near fu-
ture; and say, Amen.

May his great name be blessed, forever and ever.
Blessed, praised, glorified, exalted, extolled, honored elevated and
lauded be the Name consolations which are uttered in the world; and
say Amen. May there be abundant peace from Heaven, and life, upon
us and upon all Israel; and say, Amen."

There was comfort in Joachim's words and Reis fought back tears. Master Altschmer surprised Reis by stepping forward and reciting from some of the psalms. They lowered Jeremie's body in its grave then covered it with earth, after which Joachim said yet another prayer. His face was grim when he turned and strode back to the tent.

Four days later they still hadn't wrought the magic that Joachim was seeking. Try as he could, without the proper equipment, the scales, measures and basic ores, his skill for refining pure copper was not to come to fruition. The furnace was too rough and crudely constructed, a square structure with air holes on the sides and a mouth hole in the front. The angle was wrong, the slag built up too quickly, the metal couldn't breathe properly. It was clear he was growing frustrated and clearer still, that Pemisapan's patience was wearing thin. That they hadn't yet been killed was a miracle, Reis thought, working alongside his master and the smelter as if he were a full-grown man and not a boy. As each hour of each day passed without success, Reis sensed that Joachim's power was weakening and Pemisapan's was growing stronger. He had asked Joachim what the chief was seeking by having them refine the base ores. Joachim told him that pure copper, if he could produce it, was a rich commodity to the Savages, "like silver and gold to us, it means great wealth."

To Reis, it didn't make sense. To prefer copper over gleaming silver and shining gold was strange. But then again, the Indian ways were strange altogether; the way they spoke, oft with gestures, their clothing, even their food. As he worked alongside the two men he pondered their fate and if they would ever escape with their lives. He shuddered at Pemisapan's growing anger and envied Joachim's calm demeanor.

By now, Sir Ralph, Sir Thomas and the others must have reached the provisional camp. Had they gathered their belongings and headed downstream toward the main encampment? Would they count their losses and just be thankful that they had survived? Or might they rally a force of men to strike at the heart of the Savages, leaving Reis, Joachim and Altschmer caught in the middle? Afraid of the answers, Reis didn't ask his master any of these questions. Late one afternoon after yet another fruitless attempt, with blackened slag their only reward, Altschmer pulled Joachim to one side and spoke urgently.

"Ve must leave this place, for our lives are soon forfeit. Ist gut idea?"

Joachim shook his head. "We wouldn't get far. They would

track us easily and it would only serve to anger Pemisapan more."

Altschmer shook his head, staring solemnly at the Jew.

"Es gibt keine Magie, eh?" he muttered. "There ist no magic, eh?"

CHAPTER 19
CAN WE ESCAPE?

"WILL WE EVER get out of here?"

Joachim was studying the angle of the furnace.

"What did you say?"

"Will we get free? Do you think he'll kill us?"

Joachim shrugged.

"If I cannot produce the copper he wants, he might."

Reis gave a shudder. It wasn't the answer he was hoping for. They had been at Pemisapan's camp for two weeks now and the Great Chief came less and less frequently to the furnace site to see what Joachim and Altschmer were doing. Oft times he sent one of his councilors to check. It was an Indian called Tascon, an older man who peered, poked and prodded each time he came, running his finger over the blackened slag, feeling the impure nuggets left behind from the last roasting, shaking his head in disgust. Each time he went back to report. Then one day Tascon didn't come and they were summoned, instead, to Pemisapan's tent. Reis followed the two men with a heavy heart. He was certain this signaled their doom. It didn't seem fair. After all these days of working, Joachim and

Altschmer had produced nothing more than some small nuggets of copper defiled by the base metals from which they refused to separate themselves. He was surprised, therefore, to see the crippled chief, Menatonon waiting at the tent, with his son Skiko and two other warriors.

It was clear that Pemisapan considered Mentanon's visit an annoyance. Menatonon had come many miles to warn the chief that the English were gathering their forces. Without understanding the language, Reis sensed what he was saying: 'It was not wise to anger the English by killing their hostages. Andacon and Tarraquine would not join him. He would stand alone against the firesticks. Perhaps he should release the Magic One and his accomplice. Keep the boy if he wanted.'

All this was told to Pemisapan as the three of them stood there, watching their faces and listening to the sharp, clipped tones of their strange dialect. Reis felt Joachim's hand once again on his shoulder, the grip tight and solid. He felt Joachim's words through the muscles of his hand, 'stay calm, boy, show not your feelings.'

Pemisapan led Menatonon to the furnace by the edge of the trees, pointing out the black slag, his frustration and disgust clearly evident. Joachim tried to go with them but was stopped by his warriors. Altschmer whispered something in German and Joachim nodded. When the two chiefs came back, Menatonon turned to Joachim and said several times,

"Haarioot, Haarioot?"

Joachim shook his head and pointed south. The crippled chief understood. He spoke to Pemisapan. Reis was growing more and more scared. What if Joachim and Altschmer were forced to leave him behind? He wouldn't stay. He'd run after them. The Savages would catch him and all of Pemisapan's anger would be turned against him. He thought abruptly of Master Greutter and suddenly the world began to spin around him and he felt himself slipping....

When he came to, he was lying in the crude tent with Joachim kneeling by his side. Reis heard the Hebrew prayers and thought he was already dead. Joachim was loosening his shirt and wildly Reis thought, 'They're wrapping me in a shroud to bury me. I must surely have died.' It was only when Joachim raised his head to give him some water that he realized he could breathe more easily.

"Indeed, that was a sight," said his master with a faint smile. "The great chiefs talking and you falling to the ground."

Reis flushed.

"They think me a weakling."

Joachim shook his head.

"What they think of you does not matter. Their thoughts must be only of the three of us, for we will not leave you behind."

It was small comfort to Reis, for Joachim's words, said to assuage his fears, could offer little assurances. He and the smelter were two against many warriors armed with bows and knives. If Pemisapan so desired, he could slit their throats as easily as he'd done with Beale and Vaughan. Or he could slice them slowly, fingers, toes, ears, or gut them like a deer as he had ordered done to Greutter. As he thought like this, Reis felt the world slip away again and it was only Joachim's strong-smelling herbs that stopped his descent once more into darkness.

Menatonon left as swiftly as he arrived. He spoke at great

length to Pemisapan, then turned abruptly. As he passed Joachim he said in broken English,

"Haarioot, good man."Pemisapan was frowning as he left, the first time his face had shown any real expression. Was he frowning from news of the impending attack, or because he didn't know what to do with the two men and the boy? Was he frowning because the Magic One had failed to produce pure copper, so scarce that they had to trade with the Western tribes to get it? When would his displeasure turn to fury?

Joachim and Altschmer spoke at great length in German and, for Reis's benefit, in English as well. Reis knew Joachim was fluent in several languages, but the ease with which he conversed with the smelter was impressive. Altschmer showed none of his former hostility. Unlike Greutter, he had not appeared to carry his grudges into the enemy camp. He was greatly agitated by news of Lane's impending attack.

"Master Gans," he said in alarm, "ist this attack soon?"

Joachim shrugged.

"I do not know. Lane has had enough days to summon forces from the main camp. We must prepare…."

Altschmer coughed. When he spoke his voice betrayed his feelings.

"Master Gans,… Joachim… Greutter ist… vas… mein freund. But I hast not the anger in me that he had… Vatever you decide, I vill follow…."

Joachim silenced him with a wave of his hand.

"You are German, I am Jew. Let us not deny Teutonic hatred for my people. A man is judged by the company he keeps."

He stared at Altschmer, who dropped his eyes. "But it matters not. Ralph Lane will lead an attack against Pemisapan. Where will we be when this happens?"

"Ach," Altschmer leaned forward slightly. "Away from here far, I hope."

They gathered together what food they could find and each covered himself in an animal skin. The dark fur would blend into the shadows of the night, Joachim said, and Reis was glad of the warmth. At one point, Joachim spoke to him.

"There is danger here. If Pemisapan catches us we will most likely die. If you wish to remain behind, I will not blame you. You can wait for Lane's men to release you."

Reis shook his head. There was no way he would stay with the Savages on the chance of rescue. Once they learned of the escape, their anger would turn against the one remaining. Joachim smiled a rare smile.

"Good," he said. "I did not think you would want to stay. We will wait for nightfall then try our luck. A prayer would help."

He took from his pocket the worn and faded Holy Book he always carried, no matter what. Altschmer stared then he, too, bent his head while Joachim prayed in Hebrew. They waited until night lay heavy for several hours. The moon was full, which was not good, Joachim confirmed.

"Perhaps we should wait...."

"Nein, nein, ve must go... now, before ist too late...."

Reis was anxious to leave, too. Like Altschmer, he'd had enough of the Savages and their brutal ways. He wanted nothing more than to be far downstream safe in Ralph Lane's camp, with other soldiers and their harquebusers pointed readily at any shadow that might move.

"Can we go now, let's go now?"

Joachim frowned. The moon was too bright, casting silver light upon the earth. They would be easy to see.

"Clouds gather in the west," he said, lifting the tent flap a little and pointing to the western sky. "If a storm comes, we can leave then. The moon will be covered."

Reis's heart was racing. So what if there was a moon, they would have a head start and could surely outrun the Indians. He wished his thoughts upon Altschmer. If the big German wanted to go he would rise up also. And then Joachim would join them, moon or no moon. He closed his eyes and sent his thoughts to the smelter, 'We should go now, we should go now....'

Somehow he must have fallen asleep though he couldn't remember doing so. He awoke to Altschmer shaking him roughly.

"Get up, ist time."

Reis got up groggily. He saw Joachim standing by the tent opening, the flap pulled slightly to one side. He could see his master peering out. He could hear the rain.

Rain! Joachim has been right, as usual. With the rain to cover their footsteps and clouds to cover the moonlight, surely the Almighty was giving them a sign.

He almost rushed past Joachim in his haste to run and leave this place. He almost... and was startled to see Pemisapan walking toward their tent, the rain beating down upon his head. He was alone.

Joachim pulled him back at the last moment. He gave Reis

a shove which sent him reeling to the other side of the tent.

"Lie down," he whispered fiercely. "Pretend you are asleep."

Altschmer immediately took the hint and dropped to the ground, curling himself up as if dreaming. Joachim pulled himself back from the tent's opening and sat down quickly just as Pemisapan stepped inside. The Great Chief's eyes swept the darkness of the tent. He saw the big man and the boy asleep. He saw the Magic One sitting with his legs crossed, swaying gently from side to side. The Magic One was muttering his strange-sounding words. His hands were clasped.

Joachim stared up at Pemisapan. His eyes appeared glazed as if he had been praying for many hours. He kept swaying and muttering. The chief squatted down directly in front of him. From where he lay, Reis slowly opened one eye to see what was going on. Altschmer gave a snore and Reis almost giggled nervously. The big man groaned and stirred, then rolled over and kept snoring. But Reis knew that he, also, was wide awake, waiting to see what was going to happen next. Joachim finished his prayer and fixed his eyes upon Pemisapan.

The Great Chief gave a grunt. He held out his hand. It was a pantomime, just as Reis remembered when Uncle Allyn had grudgingly allowed them to go and see the carnival which was passing through their village. The mime, with white painted face, had acted out scenes which they understood though no costumes, props or words had been used: a man was bemoaning his fate, thrown in jail for stealing an apple; a cuckolded husband was alternately weeping tears and wringing out his kerchief, which had brought roars of laughter from the audience. Here in this darkened tent it was the same, the Savage and the Jew each pantomiming his wishes to the other: the Great Chief asking for something, the mineral man hesitating, seeking his own wish in return. Reis saw Pemisapan's extended hand and though no words had been spoken, knew exactly what he wanted. Joachim knew as well, and their lives depended upon his answer.

CHAPTER 20
JOACHIM'S MAGIC

THERE WAS NO real magic, when Reis thought about it afterwards. Altschmer had been right. There were none of a conjurer's tricks: the puff of smoke, the colored scarves, the golden coin wondrously appearing from behind the Great Chief's ear. Such tricks might have forced Pemisapan to kill Joachim out of fear. Reis had seen his reaction when his master, after one long afternoon of frustration and defeat, threw multi-colored crystals onto the dying embers of the furnace. The "whoosh" of smoke and fire, the bright tongues of blue, orange, green, red and gold which shot forth had caused the Savages to draw their knives and step alarmingly closer. Only after Joachim had showed Pemisapan the pieces in his hand, only when the chief had smelled them and hesitatingly thrown them on the fire himself, had the warriors sheathed their knives and stepped back. Pemisapan had nodded and asked for some of the "magic stones." Joachim had given up his entire supply. 'Twas a fascination to the Savages, Reis thought, watching them throw crystals on the fire long into the night.

So if this stalemate here in the darkened tent was no magic

show, then what was it? Pemisapan squatted with his hand held out for a long time. Joachim sat upon his heels, moving slowly from side to side as he always did, muttering his Hebrew words, intoning his prayers and psalms while the Great Chief waited and said nothing. Altschmer had stopped pretending to snore and lay quietly, while Reis peered through half-opened eyes not daring to move. Finally, Joachim reached into his pocket and pulled forth his torn and much-used Holy Book. He handed it to Pemisapan.

The Great Chief took the book and sniffed it carefully, as a dog is wont to sniff an unfamiliar object. He opened the pages as he had seen the Magic One do many times, as he had seen the English do with their books and maps. He stared at the strange calligraphy of the Hebrew words but, Reis knew, it wouldn't have mattered if they had been written in English. He couldn't read them. Joachim's Jewish Bible could only be read by a man who knew the Hebrew language, and where was another to be found in this wilderness land? Maybe Hariot, who was himself a scholar, but he was miles to the south with Ralph Lane and the others.

Pemisapan got up slowly and signaled Joachim to do the same. His master rose and stood facing the Indian who, with hand signals and grunts in his strange tongue, told the Magic One what he could do. Joachim and Altschmer were free to leave. They could head south to meet the other English. Joachim was to stop the mad English chief from attacking Pemisapan's camp, for there would be much bloodshed if that happened. He did not wish to kill the English. His neighboring chiefs, Andacon and Tarraquine, might yet change their minds and fight by his side. It would be a pointless battle.

Joachim signaled that the boy was to come with them. Pemisapan shook his head. The boy was to stay with him. He was valuable and the English chief would not invade the camp with the boy there. Joachim and the big man were to leave now. If not, Pemisapan could not guarantee their safety or the safety of the boy. Joachim shook his head.

Pemispan's demeanor changed. His tone became threatening. He took a step toward Joachim, who held his ground. Reis's heart was beating so fast he thought for sure they would hear it. When Joachim spoke, it was in English for Reis, then in German for Altschmer, finally in gestures and signals for the chief.

"I will not leave the boy. He belongs to me... no, he belongs to himself. He comes with me and the smelter, to seek his own fortune. I will not leave him."

Pemisapan's mouth was set in a thin hard line. He placed his hand swiftly upon his knife, the same knife which had taken the life of Beale and Vaughan. Joachim didn't move.

"You can kill me," Joachim said then. "You can kill the big man and the boy. But you will have nothing. Your chiefs will not respect you. Menatonon urges caution against the English. All you will do is anger the English chief. He has many men. You will lose."

Pemisapan drew his knife. He turned and faced Reis, who held his breath. In an instant the chief had pulled the boy to his feet and was holding the knife at his throat. Never had metal felt so cold. Reis felt the sharp blade beginning to cut his skin.

"You would kill a boy?" Joachim asked, knowing that the chief could not understand his words but only his questioning tone. He stared straight into Pemisapan's eyes. The knife remained poised against Reis's throat. Joachim looked at his apprentice.

"Cease not to pray even when the knife is laid upon thy neck."

It seemed like an eternity that they stood there, Joachim with his head held high, Pemisapan unmoving as he gripped Reis in a vise. By now Altschmer had slowly risen and was standing at the far side of the tent. He was silent as a statue is silent, unmoving and frozen in time. Reis could hardly breathe. His mouth was open and gasping like a fish, but no air flowed in and out. The knife had cut a little into his skin and he could feel its stark pain. One swift move and he would be dead like the others before him. He tried to think of a prayer to the Almighty but his mind was dull-witted.

"Our Father, who art...."
"Blessed be the meek...."

Only his heart thudding in his chest told him he was still alive. The knife cut a little deeper and Reis felt a trickle of warm blood run down his neck. He couldn't even struggle for the blade would press harder into his body. To his great horror he watched as Joachim slowly turned away, his back now facing Pemisapan.

'Oh, Joachim, why did you do that? The Great Chief's anger will surely know no bounds!'

Reis could hear the drumming of his blood, the heavy breathing of Altschmer, the murmuring of Pemisapan's fury rising, an anger visible and alive. Above even these sounds he heard Joachim's low voice saying his Hebrew prayers.

"The Lord sends death and life. He brings down to the nether-world

and brings up from it. Into Thy hand I commit my spirit; Thou wilt surely redeem me, Lord, God of Truth..."

'What prayer was this? Was Joachim resigning him to death?' Then the Jew stopped, his voice silent as he turned back to face the Savage. Pemisapan's grip was as tight as ever, the knife a stroke away from severing Reis's jugular vein. Reis felt his eyes beginning to burst their sockets. To his great shame he felt warm wetness trickling down his leg.

Then suddenly the pressure on his neck decreased, the grip loosened and he stumbled away, almost falling to the earth. He saw what Joachim was holding in his hand and drew an intake of breath. Dangling from its chain was the Magen David, the heavy silver star that Joachim had reclaimed from Greutter. Joachim was holding the Jewish symbol out, offering it to Pemisapan, offering his most prized possession in return for Reis's life.

Pemisapan sheathed his knife and took the gleaming six-pointed star. It was large and heavy and thick, of great value to anyone who knew the weight of silver, of even greater value, Reis knew, to Joachim Gans. He felt himself unworthy of such an offering yet, at the same time, was thankful beyond all belief that the Savage so desired it that he would make the trade. One silver Jewish Magen David for one thin and awkward apprentice. One piece of silver for the life of a boy who had just now pissed out his fear for all to see.

But Pemisapan didn't even notice Reis huddled near the side of the smelter, Altschmer. Nor did he notice Joachim when he wrapped the bear skin tightly around himself and signaled to them. Pemisapan's eyes were focused on the star, his hands caressing its gleaming surface, his head nodding approval. For this silver ornament, meaningless to him in its Jewish symbolism, was the Magic One's totem. With this now in his possession, the power of Pemisapan would spread far and wide. Enemies would bow down before him, victory would be his, abundance would fill his storehouses and his children would grow in power and wisdom. He was still admiring the Magen David when Joachim, Altschmer and Reis slipped out of the tent.

They ran for what seemed like miles, until Reis's heart pounded violently against his ribs. He kept glancing over his shoulder fully expecting to see the Savages in hot pursuit. Altschmer pushed him forward and he almost fell. The big man had said not a word since Pemisapan first stepped through the opening. Wrapping himself in a fur, he had thrown one over Reis's shoulders, pushing him ahead as the two of them followed Joachim quickly while the chief was dreaming his dreams of power.

Pemisapan sat lost in his own reverie, mesmerized as he caressed the silvered outline of the star. It was two inches in each direction, heavy and weighted. What was copper compared to this shining symbol? Its six points represented earth, fire, wind, water, the yellow sun, the moon and stars. Whoever possessed this talisman possessed the greatest wealth of all, power over the elements of the universe, power equal to that of the Great Spirit. How heavy around the neck of a mere man, yet how light in the knowledge of what that man wore. He could afford to let the three men go; they were nothing to him now. If the mad English chief attacked, he would be invincible, his people impervious to danger.

Pemisapan caught them leaving out of the corner of his eye

but let them pass with no thought. They were as drops of rain in a mighty tempest, insignificant against his newly-acquired amulet, that which he had coveted from the first sight of it around the Magic One's neck.

Running, running was all Reis knew, the thud of his feet on the wet ground, almost slipping on the sodden leaves. Oft times Joachim or Altschmer reached out a hand to steady him. A dull ache grew in his side until it was a bright pain. He could run no more and collapsed against a fallen tree trunk, sobbing and gasping for air.

"Wir sollten jetzt gehen. Ve must go," the smelter, too, was breathing harshly. "Before he comes after us."

"We can... rest a moment," Joachim panted, his breath coming in short gasps. "He will not follow."

"Nein, nein," urged Altschmer, trying to rise though his huge legs wouldn't budge. "He ist angry."

Joachim shook his head. He looked like a crazy wild man, Reis thought, the water streaming from his hair and beard. Only his eyes were Joachim's eyes.

"Er hat was er will," he said in German. "He has what he wants."

Altschmer stared at him for a long time. Joachim nodded to Reis.

"Can you run?"

CHAPTER 21
FLIGHT

THEY KEPT MOVING through the wind and rain. The thunder rumbled and the lightning cut huge jagged slashes in the darkness. At each crack of lightning the tops of the trees became bright as the day. The woodlands were streaked with silver. Reis glanced over his shoulder, half-expecting to see Pemisapan's warriors running through the trees after them.

They ran for miles, slipping and sliding down embankments, following the course of the big winding river. Lane's main camp lay far to the south close to that river. As long as they kept the dark waters to their right they could not miss the encampment. They ran through sodden leaves and over the roots of trees, trying not to trip and fall. The witches and demons who roamed these dark woods chuckled and pointed long bony fingers at them. Reis could swear he saw them watching, their yellow eyes burning holes in the black night, stirring their cauldrons and chanting their unholy spells.

"*Death, death,*" they moaned. "*Death is coming after you. Death is waiting, you can't escape, you can't escape....*"

They cackled in obscene laughter and the sound sent chills

racing through him. Reis could almost smell their fire and brimstone. A loud crack of thunder, an explosion of lightning and a tree, sheared in half by Hell's fury, fell just to their left. Joachim ran, his long hair flapping in the wind and the bear's skin wrapped around him giving him the appearance of a large furry beast. Altschmer cursed as tree roots caught his feet. Reis rolled down a muddy slope and landed with the breath knocked out of him. Joachim followed him down and pulled him back up the slope, the mud sucking at their ankles. They could not hear if the enemy was approaching and they didn't wait. They kept running and rested only when they could no longer breathe, doubling over in pain and moaning softly in their anguish. Above and all around them the storm raged in its fury. It was a cold drenching rain, icy and mixed with snow. As long as he kept moving Reis felt warm, but when they stopped he began shivering, his teeth chattering and his bones starting to ache.

"Ve must stop," the German called out at one point. "Ist no gut to run like this. Ve vill not make it und all Lane vill find ist our dead bodies."

Joachim nodded in agreement and they searched for an outcropping of rock, sheltered part-way from the storm's fury. Once inside, Reis flung himself down on the cold ground. He rubbed furiously at his legs but the pain wouldn't go away. He had lost his bearskin in the slide down the embankment and Joachim took off his and wrapped it over the boy's shoulders.

"What about you?" Reis asked. "You'll get sick."

Altschmer gave a hearty laugh.

"Sick? You vorry about getting sick? Ist joke? Better sick than cut to pieces."

He grew solemn and buried his face in his hands. Reis felt the big man's pain but it was his own pain that stabbed like needles through his leg muscles, that stabbed deep in his chest.

"Can we die from running so hard?" he asked Joachim. The Jew smiled faintly.

"Only if we don't run," he said.

They slept for under an hour while the storm still raged outside. They couldn't light a fire and when Joachim began shivering himself, Reis shared the bearskin. The half of him closest to his master felt warm but his other side was freezing cold. Altschmer sat with his head buried in his hands for most of the time. When at last Joachim said it was time to go, the big man shook his head.

"Ich bleibe hier."

"No," said Joachim firmly. "We go on."

Altschmer got slowly to his feet. He took a sharp stone from the ground and, tearing and pulling, separated his animal skin into two parts. One half he gave to Reis, the other he tucked under his shirt as best he could.

"Now we both keep varm," he said and pushed Reis outside.

It took them the rest of the night to find the camp. It wasn't the main camp where Ralph Lane waited but a temporary one they had used on their journey north. Joachim recognized it and Altschmer agreed. Remains of the crude furnace were still scattered on the ground and the circle of stones to contain their fire clearly marked where they had been.

"How far?" the German asked, looking south.

Joachim shrugged.

"At least thirty miles," he replied. "Maybe forty or even more."

The big man sighed.

"No more tonight," he said. "Ve are far enough avay."

He let his question trail off, not seeking an answer. If Pemisapan wanted to track them, he could. Not even the storm could thwart his warriors if they searched hard enough or ran far enough. Altschmer sat down on the cold ground and stubbornly refused to move any further.

Joachim stood guard while the big man and Reis rested. The boy couldn't sleep with the sounds of the storm raging all around. Lightning sheared the tops of the trees, thunder boomed and it was as if the Almighty Himself was delighting in showing His awesome powers.

"You think your Magen David is powerful?" God cried out. *"You are nothing, nothing to Me! I rule this world and all the Heavens. Do not presume to set yourselves above Me!"*

"No, no, You are the Creator, our God! Spare us, spare us from the heathen devils."

"You have nothing left," the wind howled around the branches. It spoke to Joachim. *"You have given away your faith. For what, a worthless boy?"*

"We shall suck the marrow from his bones," the witches chortled gleefully. *"Give him to us."* They stretched out bony arms, cackling in the wind.

"Give him to us, we will boil him alive."

Reis lay trembling under a rock, trying to keep warm, but his shivering was more from fear than cold. How could Joachim save him? The Savages would come and cut the flesh from his bones. Altschmer would be gutted just like Greutter. He could hear Greutter's screams rising and falling in the wind, "Save me, save me. Nein, nein, stop, please stop!"

He must have passed out again for he awoke to a large bear shuffling near him. The bear looked very much like his master. It had the body of a man but the head of a beast, with huge yellow eyes and gleaming teeth. What manner of creature was this? Perhaps he had died and was already in Hell. He glanced around, searching for the yellow flames. Surely he was the Devil's prize now, a useless, worthless lad with the smell of piss still on him. Piss and sweat, piss and fear, rank smells which fouled the nostrils and choked the lungs. Was he pissing again? He couldn't tell.

"Aaaaaeeeeee! Aaaaaeeeeee!"

Greutter's screams sounded in his ears. He jumped up with a start. Joachim was lumbering about in the wind and rain looking for something. What did he want? At long last he held something aloft and cried out in triumph. It was a small turnip. In his other hand he held pieces of sodden bread, leftovers from their last sojourn here, missed by the scavengers.

"We have food," he cried to the rain and wind. "We will not starve!"

Alstschmer awoke and sat up, eyes glancing all around fearfully. When he realized the cries had been Joachim's, he relaxed.

"Get up, boy," he turned to Reis. "Your master ist crazy man."

Then he laughed, a loud booming laugh rivaling the thunder, it seemed. Reis saw that the half-bear, half-man beast was only Joachim. His heart did a flip-flop in his chest and he took the moldering biscuits that Joachim thrust in his hand and ate them. To his shrunken stomach, it was manna from Heaven!

The goblins and witches howled their frustration. They

clattered bones and banged skulls together but they couldn't touch him now. He ate and then ate some more, dulling the pangs of his hunger while the hellish chorus gnashed their teeth in anger.

"*Not this time, not this time,*" they cried. "*Foiled again!*"

Bones rattled, tree branches cracked against each other, wind whistled through all the woodland spaces, the crowded bushes and overgrown grasses.

"*Foiled again,*" the witches cried out. "*But our time will come, it will come!*"

"And this," his master said, thrusting a turnip at him. "Eat, eat!"

CHAPTER 22
RALPH LANE'S CAMP

"HERE NOW," CALLED Master Lane as they stumbled upon his troops. They were already miles from the temporary camp where they'd stayed, rummaging through some packs left behind for the scraps which Joachim had found. The soggy biscuits and turnips, wet but still edible, had filled the ache in his belly and brought a warmth flooding through his body.

Joachim had kept the first watch while he and Altschmer rested. His fitful sleep had been full of the demons and painted Savages. In one, Master Greutter appeared minus his fingers, his bloody stumps reaching out to grab him. Reis had moaned, tossing and turning in his effort to escape the clutching hands. Joachim had shaken him awake and he stirred, grateful for the reprieve. But he had sunk again into a netherworld of painted men who danced around a burning fire. One of them was the Great Chief, Pemisapan, who was wearing Joachim's silver Magen David. Pemisapan had long ear curls dangling at each side of his head. He looked remarkably like the Queen's mineral man.

"Heathen," said Master Greutter, clutching his stomach

from which half his intestines dangled. "You are a heathen, no better than these devils."

Master Greutter vanished and Pemisapan/Joachim nodded his head.

"I am a heathen for Satan is my master. I know not God, nor wish to."

The Magen David melted around his neck. It ran in gleaming rivulets down his chest and dripped onto the earth.

Reis had awoken with a start. He heard Altschmer's snoring and he rose to see Joachim standing near the trees. They had lit no fire for fear of bringing attention to themselves, and the cold seeped into his bones numbing his fingers and toes. He walked to where Joachim stood.

"More bad dreams?" asked his master.

For certain, Joachim looked like a wild man. He had lost his hat in their run southward; his black hair was in disarray, the bearskin wrapped around him blended with the unkempt and fierce look. No wonder Reis had thought him a bear. No longer did he appear the gentle teacher, the astute mineral man with his measuring instruments and crucibles. No longer was he Joachim Gans, the Talmudic scholar. He looked exactly as he had appeared in Reis's dream, a wild heathen, a lumbering beast. Joachim peered quizzically at him.

"You have questions?" he commented.

"Yes," Reis blurted out.

"Then ask."

"Master, I don't wish to...."

"... offend me?"

Reis shook his head.

"You gave Pemisapan your Magen David. It was your most prized possession. You would die rather than part with it."

Joachim gave a wry smile.

"And have you die just to keep it?"

Reis stared at him. The enormity of what Joachim said weighed heavily on him. Was it possible his master had had murder in his heart that day when Greutter had stolen the star? Joachim was not a violent man but surely violence had driven his heart and soul that moment so long ago? If looks could have killed Greutter, then the German would have died on the spot. Yet he had handed the star to the Great Chief as easily as he had given him the copper crystals. Why was that? Could Reis's life mean so much to him?

"Aah," said Joachim, a smile tracing his mouth. "You ask what is the value of one young boy? How do you measure up to the weight of silver?" He shrugged. "Maybe it was a poor bargain."

He turned to face the woods.

"Go back to sleep. Like the Talmud says, your head is as solid as iron, so perhaps I am not such a good teacher after all. When you have figured out the proper question, you will also know its answer."

Three days later they saw Lane and his harquebusiers through the trees. The soldiers were scouting well ahead of Amadas, Hariot and the others. Reis cried out in his gladness at seeing them. Altschmer stumbled ahead waving his arms. He was a fearsome sight, the animal skin flapping from his shirt, his eyes wild. He lumbered toward them like a bear and one of the harquebusiers raised his musket to take aim.

"Nein, nein!" he cried, ripping the fur from him. "Altschmer, ist Altschmer!"

The soldier looked at Lane and lowered his firearm. Altschmer collapsed on the ground, half-laughing, half-moaning. Reis came next out of the trees to Master Lane, who stood staring incredulously at the bear-like man, the white-faced ragged boy. Then Joachim appeared.

"Here now, Yougham," called Ralph Lane, striding forward. "For certain, we thought you lost. We did not expect to see you alive."

Joachim walked into the midst of them and the soldiers lowered their muskets. Reis looked back at the trees, half-expecting Savages to appear. Even now, back with Lane's men, he could not feel sure Pemisapan's warriors hadn't followed them all this distance.

"Where are they?" Lane asked. "What headstart did you have? You there... and you...."

He pointed to the right, the left, and harquebusiers ran to cover the trees.

Reis shivered. Perhaps Joachim was wrong, after all. Perhaps Pemisapan even now was stringing his bow and aiming directly at his heart. Joachim had told Altschmer that the Savages wouldn't follow. How could he be so sure?

They waited for Hariot and the others to catch up. During that time, Reis ate his fill and wrapped himself in thick blankets. One of the soldiers lent him an extra jacket. Altschmer talked to anyone who would listen, telling them about Greutter and what had happened. He ate and talked, laughing and waxing sad alternately. And through all this Ralph Lane spoke with Joachim Gans, questioning him about Pemisapan. Had Tarraquine and Andacon joined forces with him yet? How many warriors had he gathered together since they were freed?

When at last Amadas, Hariot, Stafford and others joined their group, there was again a re-telling of how they'd survived and how they'd managed to escape. Altschmer started to tell the story of the silver star but a look from Joachim silenced his tongue. The smelter shrugged. Let the Jew keep his secret, no matter, they were free!

Reis basked in the men's rapt attention. He was a hero in their eyes and thus, enjoyed every moment of it. But he, too, said nothing about the Magen David. If Joachim wanted no one to know, so be it.

They rested for the night, their camp fires burning brightly. Reis chose a place close to the flames, allowing himself the luxury of feeling hunger and cold creep from his body to be replaced by fullness and warmth. The next dawn they were up and ready to go before the sun had risen. Master Lane was for sending Reis back to the south camp, for this was a raiding expedition, he stated firmly, "not fit for a boy." It was Joachim who spoke and said, "Let him stay. He has seen more than his share."

Master Hariot nodded his head and so Reis found himself once more apprenticed, this time not to work metals but to keep the powder and wicks at the ready for all who would need them.

Ralph Lane's plan was simple and straightforward. When they reached Pemisapan's camp they would spread out and surround it to attack from all sides. There would be no room for negotiation, Master Lane said, for this was to avenge the deaths of Beale, Vaughan and now, Master Greutter and Jeremie. The attack would be at night when the enemy was sleeping. The English would be able to distinguish themselves from the Savages by pulling their shirttails out in the back. It was a method used effectively by the Spanish, who called it a "camisado."

By the time they arrived on the hillside overlooking Pemisapan's camp, it had taken five more days. They quickly dispersed, with Lane sending some men to the surrounding hills, there to lie in wait for his signal. They kept themselves well-hidden from any foraging parties. Lane sent Hariot, Amadas and Stafford to reconnoiter, marking the lay of the land and the places where Pemisapan's men hunted. They avoided the open spaces which provided no cover and the marshy areas wherein their muddy footprints might reveal their presence.

Expectancy was in the air. Back now with the main group of harquebusiers and Lane himself, Reis felt a sense of exhilaration. The fear which had pervaded his being for so long had vanished. He carried the heavy powder sacks hardly feeling their weight, and kept the wick fire burning at all times, shielding it with his hands as he ran. He was glad to be there with them instead of back at the southern camp, and grateful for Joachim for speaking on his behalf.

As he ran with the men Reis noticed changes in them, imperceptible changes but there, nonetheless. Altschmer stayed close to Master Haring and the others, his grief buried deep within. He said little and smiled even less. Ralph Lane burned with a zeal which bordered on fanaticism. He spoke of nothing else but revenge, "To teach these Savages a lesson they will never forget." With wild words he rallied the harquebusiers, those incensed at the news of Valentine Beale's death, to a breaking point. They had stripped and cleaned their weapons, checked the mechanisms over and over, polished their boots to a shine and were ready for anything. Most of them were either Beale's age or a few years older. They turned pale at how he and Captain Vaughan had died, then squared their shoulders and followed Lane's every order. Even Joachim was different. He was less argumentative now, more deeply reflective than before, and his hand kept going up to the bare place on his chest where the Magen David had rested. His fingers traced over an invisible star as if it were still there, his lips moved in silent prayers of the Talmud or unknown Hebrew incantations, and he kept Reis close to his side.

They settled in their hidden spots, nestled deep within the trees, under fallen trunks, in clumps of briar thickets, there to wait until the sun went down and the enemy fell asleep. Their fires would burn low until only embers glowed; the Savages on watch would feel their eyelids growing heavy. Only the great Pemisapan might be awake, listening for any untoward sound, the crack of a twig, the rustle of a leaf. So might he sit in his chief's tent, watching the sparks from his fire, stroking and caressing the silver amulet that made him invincible, thinking of victories yet to be. But they would be false dreams, false moments of glory. It would be too late; the battle would be joined, the Savages caught unaware. Victory would be Lane's and vengeance, too, for the deaths of his men!

CHAPTER 23
THE ATTACK

SO MANY MEN died! Pemisapan's guards were the first.

"Christ, our victory!" Lane called out and the shooting began. The young harquebusiers fired round upon round. Reis was running back and forth giving them the powder sacks, lighting their wicks from his. The smell of gunpowder filled the air and rose in bluish clouds around the men. War whoops echoed from the enemy below as their guards were caught unawares, and they first realized what was happening. They stumbled out of their sleep to meet an iron ball in the chest or be faced with hand to hand combat by Lane's men. Whistling arrows sped through the air and when they contacted with human flesh, a "thwump" was heard, a gasp and moan, and a man fell mortally wounded. Joachim kept Reis low to the ground even as he ran to supply each man, for Joachim ran with him.

"Aren't you afraid?" Reis asked his master as an arrow struck the tree in front of them. "I am."

"The Lord sends death and life," Joachim replied. *"When the dust shall return to the earth that it was, the spirit shall return to God who gave it."*

"So you're not afraid?"

"Life is a passing shadow, say the Scriptures.... *Even as the shadow of a bird in its flight, it passeth from our sight, and neither bird or shadow remains.*"

"But...."

"I am cautious," panted Joachim, his wild hair flying. "I do not seek the arrow, nor wish it to seek me."

Together they helped prime the muskets, setting them up for the next round. One young harquebusier reminded Reis of Valentine Beale; he was about twenty-two with a thick thatch of brown hair and piercing blue eyes.

"What's your name?" he asked as the boy helped light the wick.

"Reis Courtney."

"I thought you be his son," and he nodded in Joachim's direction.

"He's my master and I, his apprentice. That be Master Gans, the best mineral man of the Queen."

"He looks like a wild man," laughed the soldier, "now back away," and he aimed and fired the musket. The recoil made him stagger just a little. He peered through the cloud of blue smoke.

"Did you hit anything?"

"'Course I did. I got one right smack in the head."

Reis wondered if Pemisapan was already dead, caught in the crossfire of Lane's men on the surrounding hills. But he had no time to dwell on it for Joachim was pushing him fast toward the protection of the trees.

"Don't stand out in the open talking like a fool," admonished his master. "Or shall an arrow seek you out?"

Lane was directing his men to advance upon the camp. Several soldiers volunteered to lead the others. Philip Amadas led one group and Lane the other. A third was called to scout to the left, with Edward Stafford at its command. Several harquebusiers remained behind in case the enemy crept up to catch them unaware. Joachim and Reis rested for a few moments. Nearby, Altschmer and Haring were busy priming some of the muskets.

"Go and assist them," Joachim ordered. "I will help this man."

Reis saw that the young harquebusier with the brilliant blue eyes had been wounded in the shoulder. It must have happened just after he'd fired his weapon, for the wound was bleeding profusely.

"Will he be all right?" Reis whispered. The young soldier's face was pale.

"He will live, if that's what you mean. But you can be no help here. Go now and see what you can do for the others. And keep your head low."

The young musket man whose name, Reis learned later, was Will Needles, was propped up against a tree trunk, Joachim deftly removed the arrow head with his knife while Needles bit down on a piece of wood. Blood spurted, then quickly stopped. The shoulder was bound and he staggered to his feet.

"I'm ready," he smiled wanly. "Bring on them bloody Savages," and promptly fainted. Joachim propped him up against the tree again.

"He will rest for a while."

Below them they could hear the cries of the enemy, the

yells of soldiers, the "whoosh" of the arrows winging through the air, the sharp retort of the muskets. There were several moments when all was quiet and Reis wondered if the battle was ended and who had won. Master Altschmer came over. Reis saw that his head was bleeding from a scalp wound.

"You're shot!"

"An arrow came und took a piece of my skin, that ist all. No matter, my head spins but I am still here."

He made a face.

"Never ist var gut, for ve haf dead und they do, too."

He pointed and Reis saw several bodies of young soldiers lying on the ground, arrows protruding from them. He wondered how many of Pemisapan's warriors were also lying on the ground. Then they heard Ralph Lane shout, "Over here. I need some men. Come quickly!"

Without thinking Reis ran in the direction of the cry. Joachim followed, then Altschmer and some of the harquebusiers, including an Irish soldier called Edward Nugent. They saw Sir Ralph pointing into the woods and caught a faint movement.

"Was ist los?" Altschmer called out just as others arrived.

"Pemisapan," Master Lane said, out of breath. "Just now he ran into the trees. I shot at him and would follow but I'm wounded."

Reis saw that he had an arrow protruding from his thigh. Hariot strode up to him and said.

"I will pull it out, if you wish."

"Do it."

It was impossible to pull the arrow out cleanly for the barbed head tore flesh as it was tugged backwards. Master

Lane cried out in anguish but the arrow was soon held aloft by Sir Thomas. They bound cloth around the wound to staunch the bleeding.

"That will have to be cauterized," Joachim remarked.

"Later," said Ralph Lane, struggling to stand. "We have unfinished business."

A volley of shots was heard to the left and several of the soldiers ran to assist. There were only a few of them remaining.

"I'll go," said Hariot.

"And I, too," said Altschmer. Edward Nugent went with them, his musket at the ready. Lane wished them good luck. Reis watched them walk cautiously toward the trees, then disappear into the woods.

"How many Savages are there?" Joachim asked.

"Only Pemisapan and one other that I saw. The rest are either dead or fighting on the far side."

They waited for a long time. By now, dawn's red was streaking the sky. Lines of blood snaked their way out from the horizon, with each succeeding minute growing lighter. Later came the gold. It was, Reis thought, a beautiful sunrise if one didn't think of the dead and the dying. Sir Thomas and the other two had been gone a while. Then Joachim stood up and declared that he, too, would enter the woods to see what was happening.

"If you go, then I will go," Reis blurted out.

"Nonsense," snapped Master Lane. "'Tis no place for a boy."

"This boy," said Joachim with his eyes flashing, "heard Greutter's death cries and he will come with me."

Lane stared at both of them.

"Hariot and the German are probably dead. I know not about the harquebusier, Nugent. What serves to have you go to your deaths as well?"

Joachim picked up Lane's musket.

"Help me prime this," he said to Reis.

Together they loaded powder into the firearm and Reis held the burning wick.

"Are you ready?"

"I am," Reis said determinedly, wishing he felt as strong as the words he uttered. They began to walk toward the dark trees.

"You can turn back," Joachim said, at one point stopping to look at Reis, who shook his head.

"You are a foolish boy."

Reis felt his stomach begin to churn. Perhaps he was foolish, indeed, to follow his master into these dismal woods. Who knew what they would find? Who knew whether Pemisapan was waiting for the very next English to walk into his trap? He swallowed hard and followed his master for he couldn't let Joachim go alone. Whatever they faced, it would be together. Deep in the woods' blackest heart, he heard the witches and demons chuckling, clicking their bones against each other as they waited for him.

There was no sunlight, no dawn's brilliant rays illuminating the darkness. The trees formed a canopy of black over their heads, the branches snapped against each other. He could barely see the shape of his master before him. But he could hear Joachim's breathing and his own tremulous breaths. The ground was sodden and thus, it was easy to step quietly, making no sound. Reis noticed that few birds trilled in the trees. Were they just waking up themselves?

He carried the lighted wick carefully, shielding its diminutive flame. Joachim would need him quickly if he saw Pemisapan. Where was he? The Savage hiding in the forest, waiting, waiting, made him tremble. No doubt, if caught, the torture would be unbearable.

Joachim stopped so abruptly that Reis almost bumped into him. The mineral man turned with a sharp "shsss," and Reis didn't say a word. Something was moving in the trees ahead. Something was coming toward them. Something....

"What is this?" asked Hariot, striding forward out of the dark woods. "Are you come to save us?"

He smiled and behind him came Altschmer, his huge shape lumbering to keep up. Edward Nugent followed a short distance back.

"Ist possible? You vud fight bare-hand?"

Reis glanced down at his own hands, empty save for the lighted wick. Altschmer was right. The only weapon they had between them was the harquebuser, and that was good for one shot at a time. If they missed, or if Pemisapan went down and his companion came lunging from behind a tree, what would Joachim have done? What would he have done? Perhaps he was very foolish. And perhaps his master was equally foolish, with his mind only on prayer and quotes from the Talmud, certainly not on reality. He hung his head and reddened under their gaze.

But Joachim held his head high and stared directly at Master Altschmer. He handed him the musket.

"I knew it was not needed," he said quietly.

"Ach," replied the smelter, "ist gut thing."

Both Hariot and Altschmer bore signs of a violent struggle.

Their clothing was ripped and each had wounds. Altschmer's head was gashed again and one of his eyes puffed and swollen shut. Hariot was clutching his arm, where red splayed out and trickled down to his wrist.

"No mind," said Hariot, catching their gaze. "'Tis nothing but needs a good bandage and a poultice of Joachim's medicinal herbs for my arm and my friend here."

"Perchance a stitch or two," murmured Joachim.

Just then as Edward Nugent came up, he produced from behind his back the head of the Great Chief, severed at the neck, its eyes still open and staring sightlessly at Reis. The Great Chief Pemisapan swung harmlessly in the young Irish soldier's hand, blood still oozing.

"What a sight, eh?" he said with a smile and strode past Joachim and Reis, past Hariot, out of the trees and up the slope toward Sir Ralph who was hobbling down, dragging his leg behind him. They turned and followed him. From the deep dark woods behind him, Reis heard the demons and witches from Hell moaning and grumbling their disappointment. Dead bones, or maybe it was just dead branches, rattled and cracked against each other and the wind sighed restlessly.

"Too bad, too bad," they cried. *"But sleep not soundly. Our turn will come, just wait and see. Next time... next time...."*

There was much rejoicing in Lane's camp that night. They had declared an open victory, searched out the lesser chiefs and weroances, rounded up those still alive, along with the women, children and old men. With Hariot translating, they were warned of what would happen again if the English were attacked. Lane's men ransacked whatever food they could from the remaining unburned storehouses and marched up the hill and down the far side, carrying the bodies of those who'd had the misfortune to be killed. Before they left, however, Master Altschmer walked up to Joachim and handed him something which glistened in the early light of morn.

"This ist for you," the smelter said, thrusting it into Joachim's hand. His master stared down at the Magen David. He rubbed the bloodstains off and held it up to the light for all to see. The thick silver amulet of the Jew caught a thin ray of sun and gleamed brightly.

"Ist gut thing, ja?"

Joachim slowly fastened the star around his neck. He brought it up to his lips and kissed the six points of light. Then Sir Thomas Hariot handed him the other gift, the worn and much-used Holy Book of Prayer, also taken from Pemisapan. Reis saw that Joachim's eyes were shining with tears.

"Master...?" he began.

"Aber nein," said Altschmer, pulling him away. "He saved my life und yours, now he hast back that vich he sacrificed. Come avay."

CHAPTER 24
"TELL YOUR MASTER...."

ALTSCHMER'S ONLY REGRET was that they couldn't find Master Greutter's body to bury it. He searched the edges of the woods and deep into the trees, hoping he would stumble upon the corpse of his friend. But the scavengers had gotten there first and nothing remained. It was the first and only time Reis saw the big man weep; when he stumbled out of the trees his eyes were red. But he quickly brushed aside any concern and went about his job of helping the others gather up the dead.

Joachim cauterized Ralph Lane's wound. It was a fearsome thing to see the red hot iron held against the raw flesh and listen to the cries of their leader as he was held down, watching the smoke rising from the blistered edges.

"Damnation, Yougham," groaned Master Lane and promptly fainted. But it was the only way to prevent infection, Joachim said. Lane came around to find the Jew bandaging his leg. A makeshift stretcher was constructed and though he wanted to walk, he was laid upon it protesting mightily. The wounded were tended to as best they could, several arrow heads pulled, a knife wound closed, even a metal ball dug from someone's shoulder, accidentally shot by one of their own men in spite of the white shirt tail showing. Altschmer shook his head at the offer of Joachim's help, then relented and let him cleanse the wound and apply his herbs. The Irish soldier, Edward Nugent, was a hero to them all, having hacked off Pemisapan's head, placing it on the ground before Master Lane.

"Na creacha an chogaidh," he gave a hearty laugh. "The spoils of war."

It took them several days to leave the territory of the Savages and feel confident enough to make camp. For two days and nights they rested while the wounded got stronger. Lane's decision to bury the dead there was applauded by all. It had been arduous to carry the bodies of their fallen comrades. Graves were dug and each body carefully interred. A wooden cross was placed atop each fresh pile of earth and prayers for their souls were said.

Reis wondered if Joachim would say the prayers that he had recited over Jeremie to bring comfort, but no one asked. Not much had changed, he thought. The weary soldiers stayed by themselves; Haring and Altschmer talked together; Lane, Hariot, Amadas and Stafford further discussed strategies, while Joachim remained alone. He waved Reis away with a careless gesture when the boy ventured near. He slept farthest away from the camp fire and ate by himself. Even after Master Hariot called him over, he shook his head and stayed isolated. Reis couldn't understand why he chose to remain so apart.

They rested yet another day then continued their journey south. Ralph Lane refused the stretcher and forced himself to walk, though he was stiff and his leg pained him greatly. He and Hariot conferred constantly on their situation and what would happen next. According to Lane, their supplies back at the main camp were dangerously low. The Savages, upon hearing the news of their battle with Pemisapan, had withdrawn and there was no sight of any who inhabited the areas through which they were traveling.

"Ist not gut?" Altschmer asked Sir Thomas. The great astronomer shook his head.

"It is both good and bad. Good that they don't confront us. Bad that they are now wary to the point that should we need provisions, we will fare badly without their help."

Reis remembered that when they'd first arrived, some of Manteo's people had come from their island far to the south with offers of food. And even Pemisapan, while he still called himself Wingina and was friendly toward them, had shown them how to construct the weirs and plant vegetables. Now their food was almost depleted and the Savages showed no inclination to share further. Sir Richard Grenville had left for England in August, promising a speedy return with supplies. Winter crossings were harsh and hazardous. There had been no sign of any ships.

For some strange reason, Reis was eager to see young Hugh Salter. The boy had not been on his mind these many months but with Jeremie's death, he found himself more alone, wishing for companionship. Joachim had shut him out again; the wall built by the Jew was as high as ever. Hoping to please his master, he tried to anticipate his needs and only succeeded in angering him. Reis thought of Hugh at the southern camp under the harsh tirade of Master Snelling and almost envied him. At least Hugh hadn't seen what he'd seen, nor heard the cries of a man tortured and begging for mercy. He wondered if Hugh would notice whether he'd changed much. He had changed, he knew it, as surely as the seasons changed from summer to autumn, to winter, to spring. It was not so much physical, though his shirt was tighter and his trousers shorter, but it was in his mind that the changes lay. Life, which had once seemed so simple, was now a complicated matter. Master Greutter's death hung heavy upon him.

He thought he knew Death well until the Savages dragged the miner off into the trees. Death became even more personal when he saw Jeremie's thin body lying on the ground, and the bodies of the young soldiers buried in wilderness earth. Death, the eager visitor who rubbed His bony hands together, the specter from the past, now peered over his shoulder and followed his footsteps.

Life was more complicated in other ways, too. Altschmer had become more withdrawn, much like his own master. The two rarely spoke, though they had worked side by side at Pemisapan's camp. Altschmer had given Joachim the Magen David, whereas he could have left it lying on the blood-soaked earth. Joachim had taken it with a slight nod of his head.

This, and working together at the enemy's makeshift furnace should have brought them closer somehow, but they were not. If anything, Altschmer kept as far away from Joachim as possible and he, from the smelter. Reis couldn't understand why.

He liked the smelter more than before, perhaps for his few acts of kindness and for showing the weakness of tears

As for Joachim, for whom his admiration knew no bounds, he emulated him still and wanted to learn more about the mystical Hebrew religion. Joachim was always quoting sayings from the Talmud and each story enforced Reis's belief that the Jews, far from being Christ killers and drinkers of human blood as history had so painted them, were as one with The Creator and all living things, men of peace and prayer.

'Perhaps I have become the sieve after all,' Reis thought, 'learning what is most important and letting the grains of uselessness wash away.'

It was a poetic image and Reis, never thinking himself a poet by nature or station, was fascinated by the concept.

They reached the main camp within three weeks, for they couldn't move as fast as they'd have liked. One young soldier, thankfully not Will Needles, died of his wound's infection along the way and they buried him and marked the grave with yet another cross.

The soldiers and craftsmen left behind crowded around upon their return, questioning about their explorations and learning quickly enough of Pemisapan's death. A sober Hugh Salter approached Reis and inquired after Jeremie. Reis felt a choking in his throat when he told what had happened. Hugh Salter paled at the news.

"I'm glad I didn't go," he said finally. "I would put up with a thousand Master Snellings...."

He left the sentence unfinished but Reis knew. Not even threats of a whipping could compare to the ferocity he'd seen. He felt so much older than the boy standing before him, not in the measure of years but in all things. Hugh's lower lip began to quiver and Reis saw he was fighting not to cry. He turned away abruptly and left Hugh to his misery. There was no point to tears. He had learned that long ago and nothing had happened to make him think otherwise.

He wandered over to Altschmer and Haring. The big man seemed glad enough to see him, even offering some food. For want of a better place to go, Reis sat down and began to eat.

"He ist gone und I miss him," Altschmer said slowly. "Erhart vas a bitter man, full of hate, but he vas mein freund."

Haring nodded.

"Und so geht das Leben," he said in German.

Altschmer looked at Reis.

"How ist Master Gans? I hast not seen him."

Reis shrugged.

"He's busy with Sir Thomas, I suppose."

Altschmer got up slowly.

"Tell your master… that Hans Altschmer… thanks him."

Reis went to Joachim's tent to find him poring once more over his journal, writing copious notes. When he told Joachim what the smelter had said, his master replied, "I did nothing."

Reis watched his master labor over his notes. This time they were in German.

"Why don't you write in Hebrew?" he asked.

"For the scientific terms, German is best."

"Master Altschmer is grateful to you," he repeated.

It was a bold thing to say. Joachim shrugged.

"I did nothing," he said again.

"You saved our lives, mine and his. And yours as well."

Joachim peered at him with burning eyes.

"You think I did it to save Altschmer's life?"

"Didn't you?"

Reis's face was red but still he persisted.

"Didn't you want to save his life?"

Joachim hesitated for but a moment.

"He is a German. He hates the Jews, it is part of his blood. You are English and foolish. That is your misfortune. I did it to save myself."

He closed his notebook with finality.

"Do you believe me?"

Reis slowly shook his head. Oh, why couldn't he ever get Joachim to say what he really meant, instead of speaking in these riddles?

CHAPTER 25
THE MEASURE OF A MAN

SIR THOMAS AND Joachim went over their journals comparing each to the other's. Sir Thomas's notes contained a record of their exploration; the paths they took, the rivers they crossed, the topography, the plant and animal life, the types of rock-face were all a part of his work. Reis watched them both.

"This is incomplete," he frowned. "When we return to England I shall elaborate further to give a true historical account of our discoveries."

"Why must you write more, Sir Thomas?"

"For the Queen's knowledge, boy, and for Sir Ralegh whose monies financed our journey. They are anxious to know if these lands are worthwhile to pursue." He paused. "Indeed, I feel this to be true and am of the opinion that they are rich beyond measure, if not in gold, silver and copper, then surely in land and timber for settlement and the building of England's navy."

Joachim's writings, on the other hand, were scientific in nature and written in the different languages he knew. There were intricate diagrams and drawings of rock formations, sketches of furnaces and instruments. Reis had no idea what some of the diagrams represented. Arrows pointed this way and that, uniting things together in a chemical language which, his master said, represented how the substances combined.

"This, for instance, is chalcocite," and he pointed to some strange symbols written down. Reis could make no sense of it. Joachim explained about other copper alloys such as azurite and malachite, and though Reis tried hard to comprehend the relationship of one to the other as they joined together to form a new substance, it was all too abstract!

"If you wish to be a mineral man, you must learn these things," Joachim noted, though Reis thought later that perhaps he should not consider becoming one if it meant having to memorize and understand all the complicated diagrams. Writing down what made up each substance was as difficult as learning his master's Hebrew language.

The men hunted as often as they could to supplement their meager supplies, but the deer had hidden themselves away deep in the surrounding forests. They occasionally caught rabbits, small grouse and squirrels. It was hardly enough to feed all of them. Reis and Hugh were sent to the small streams and the big river, there to crack the ice at the edges and drop their lines. Several weirs were constructed and those were successful. When the temperature rose somewhat and the sluggish fish awoke from their sleep, they swam stupidly into the weirs to make a tasty supper later. And so the winter rounded into spring.

There was no more metal ore burned, no more roasting and scooping off the regulus, no more of measuring and weighing. Their energies were put to gathering food for their survival and waiting for the relief ships which hadn't come. Each day the lookouts rowed downstream to search for signs of a ship on the sound, a ship from England which had braved the mighty seas and come with their much-needed supplies. The men's spirits sank lower and lower as their tempers grew meaner.

Throughout this time, Reis worked each morn with Altschmer and Haring, helping them set the snares or else, he went with Hugh to check the weirs and gather firewood. Each afternoon he sat near Master Gans and, while on the pretext of trying to read his Holy Book, took measure of the man working next to him. He had asked Joachim for the book, hoping there would be an English translation next to each prayer. But it was all in Hebrew. Joachim offered to teach him some of the letters.

"This means Shalom," he said, pointing to the symbol. "It is the word for peace. And this means the Shabbat, our Holy Day."

But try as he might, Reis couldn't remember the differences. He studied the man instead, the angles and lines of his face, the movement of his hands whether at writing or prayer, the dull morose quality of his eyes where once they had flashed fire. He imagined a young boy learning at his father's side, going to the Holy Temple to worship, reading Judaic writings earnestly by the flickering light of candles. No climbing trees or boyish pranks for the young Joachim. Only studious thoughts and reflections that marked the passage of his youth. And now it was true, also, Joachim had changed the way he had changed, the way Altschmer had changed. Joachim was now less argumentative. But if that were a good thing, it was balanced by his deeper introspection. He spoke only to Sir Thomas and ignored the others, including Master Lane. He remained mainly in his tent, not even going to the edges of the trees to pray the way he used to do. He was not concerned with the search for food, taking whatever Reis brought him as long as it wasn't meat. One evening he summoned Reis to his side. The boy came wondering whether his master wished his boots cleaned or was going to lecture him on Talmudic wisdom.

"You are thin," Joachim remarked. "Are you eating?"

Reis nodded that he was, indeed, eating but there simply wasn't enough food. Joachim said, "You can catch fish?"

"Not many, truly. The waters are still cold and they're hard to find."

"So fish sleep in winter like the bears?"

He looked up and smiled at Reis. It was a rare moment and one the boy hadn't seen in a long time. He sat down and studied his master's face. Since he had lost his hat, Joachim's head remained uncovered and he hadn't pulled his long hair back. He looked as much a wild man as ever, with the dangling ear curls and his thick beard. Reis suddenly realized that Joachim wasn't an old man at all, but his clothing and appearance made him seem aged beyond his years.

"Master," Reis began. It was difficult to say what was on his mind.

"Go on."

"We have suffered many losses...."

"This journey was not without its dangers."

"I miss... I...." He stumbled over the words, not knowing how to speak his thoughts clearly. Joachim interrupted.

"The boy should not have died. That was your fault."

His master's words were harsh to his ears. He knew Joachim spoke the truth but the pain was no less. He hung his head.

"Yet you can be forgiven your transgression, for the Almighty is merciful to the young."

"Where is Jeremie now?"

Joachim's brows arched above his dark eyes.

"You doubt he is with God?"

"I want to believe that he is."

"Then it is true."

"And... Master Greutter?"

Joachim shrugged. "Master Greutter's fate is unknown."

"Will a ship ever come for us?"

"That, too, is unknown. But," and he rose, "I believe it will, for your Queen is anxious for news about these lands."

Reis swallowed hard, gathering his courage.

"There is one more question...."

Joachim stood, swaying side to side. His fingers played with the silver star and he began to mumble a Hebrew prayer.

"... Why did you wait so long... to give Pemisapan the Magen David? If you had given it sooner, perhaps... perhaps...."

Oh, that the Almighty should strike him dead for such insolence! Reis held his breath and heard Joachim sigh deeply. The Jew walked to the opening of the tent and faced the stark trees, still bare from winter's icy grip.

"Could I have saved him? ... Did I wish it so...?"

He turned to look at Reis and his face was a mask the boy could not read. Joachim sighed, *Thou wilt surely redeem me, Lord, God of Truth. And the Lord will wipe away the tear from every face....*

Leaving Joachim, Reis was as confused as ever. Did this mean that Joachim was truly sorry for what happened to Master Greutter? Would Pemisapan have killed him as the sacrificial lamb no matter what Joachim had done? It was all such a puzzlement with no answers forthcoming. Rather than seeking Hugh, he went instead to Sir Thomas's tent. The great man was gathering his notes together.

"How is your master?"

"He is a mystery to me," Reis answered fretfully. "I think I understand him less and less."

Sir Thomas smiled.

"Joachim Gans has many mysteries. As a Jew he is complex, for they are a complex people. But he is also very human. He has much to think about and to come to terms with."

"Master Greutter's death?"

"That, and his own self. He is a man torn in many directions. However, he speaks highly of you, young Reis. You should be flattered."

"He's never said so to me."

"Ah," Sir Thomas smiled. He walked over to Reis and placed his hands upon the boy's shoulders.

"Joachim would not say it to your face. But he has spoken of keeping you on as his apprentice. Surely that is reason enough to believe he holds you in high regard."

He turned to go.

"Now I must speak with Ralph Lane. Sails have been sighted on the far horizon. They do not come a moment too soon, for we are close to starvation without supplies. The dispositions of the men grow ugly as their bellies grow empty. In less than a week we will leave and Lane and I must prepare now a report for Walter Ralegh. What we have discovered here can render a new settlement economically sound, thus ensuring its permanence."

"So there will be another colony?"

"Indeed," replied Sir Thomas with a smile, "if Master Ralegh has his way. In spite of our sad losses, another colony will come with women and children to make of these lands a true home."

Sad losses! A thought of Valentine Beale and his friend, Jeremie, crossed Reis's mind. But there was no time for reflection. He ran quickly to Hugh Salter to tell him the news. The boy began jumping up and down excitedly.

"Sails? Did you say sails, truly?"

"What's this," called Master Snelling. "Has my young apprentice lost his wits? Come now, there is work to be done."

Reis left Hugh with his master and ran back to Joachim's tent.

"Did you hear the news. Ships have been sighted on the far horizon. We'll be leaving soon. You'll need to gather all your equipment."

Joachim stared at him for a long time.

"Master, aren't you glad? We are to be rescued."

"For, indeed, we have all been lost."

Reis waited until Joachim's eyes focused once more upon him.

"Master...," he began.

"You asked me once a question, boy, to seek an answer. Do you remember? But it was the wrong question."

He peered more closely at Reis, his eyes bright and penetrating.

"Think. What should you have asked me?"

What did Joachim mean? Was it about Master Greutter? Was it about learning the science of metals? Had it to do with Jeremie's death? Another riddle?

How he hated riddles. They had always perplexed him and made him the target for others' laughter. He couldn't fathom the twisting of words, taking their convoluted meanings to make something entirely different.

"No sooner spoken, than broken. What is it?" shouted his oldest cousin, Thomas. Reis just stood there, angry with himself, clenching his fists.

"A secret, you dullard!" Thomas was laughing loudly. "At night they come without being fetched. By day they are lost without being stolen?"

Reis walked away while Thomas shouted, "The stars, you blockhead!"

The cries echoed behind him, "Blockhead, blockhead!" while all the cousins howled with glee and so he turned, rushing up to Thomas. He swung his fist and hit his cousin squarely in the jaw. Thomas fell down in the dirt then ran crying to his mother. The aunt whipped Reis soundly and sent him to bed without any supper. He was sore for days but it was worth it, for afterwards Thomas stayed far away with a great purple bruise on the side of his face, a split lip and a missing tooth..

Yes, riddles were a torment to him and he turned to go, his head down, then felt Joachim's grip upon his shoulder and his voice whispering in his ear.

"Think, boy, think. Only use the brain God blessed you with. You once questioned the measure of a man against the weight of silver. You asked why I didn't give the Magen David sooner and I have no answer for you." He sighed. "I did not give it up for Greutter... I could not... yet is one life of more value than another?" He sighed again. "Most assuredly, that will be a torment to me all my days. Master Greutter thought I was magic. Do you think it so?"

There it was again, the riddle of magic, the conjurer's magic, the sleight of hand, the shining crystals shooting colored flames into the air. No, wait... This was not the magic Joachim meant, the outward show of illusion and witchery, of demon and phantasm. It was something inside perhaps, oh just beyond his grasp, taunting him, mocking him. Could it have to do with silver stars and faith and God? Reis was all puzzlement as he stood in front of his master while Joachim waited, waited....

And then suddenly he knew. It was as if the grey fog clouding his brain all these weeks had been swept away in a bright wind and he knew, he knew what his master was asking. He turned to Joachim and his heart was beating hard against his ribs.

"I know the question," he said with a boldness. "It isn't the measure of silver and its weight, is it?"

Joachim waited patiently.

"What is faith, truly?"

The Jew nodded and now his fingers ran the edges of the star, tracing its outline.

"And the answer?"

The scene with Pemisapan flashed before Reis's eyes, the stoic war chief waiting, the solemn Jew dangling the silver star before him, the game played out to its very last moment Too late for Greutter who could not have been saved no matter what Joachim did or did not do, for surely his own actions had condemned him.

"It never truly mattered that Pemisapan had your star, for in giving it up you did not give up your faith. That which you treasure most can never be taken from you. Faith in one's heart can't be sold or bartered away. Faith is the measure of a man, not silver or gold."

"And the Magen David?"

"You are a man of God with or without it. For that is what you are, always."

There was a silence broken only by the sound of Reis's heart thumping against his ribs and the long drawn-out sigh of his master. Reis saw a solitary tear trace its way down the Jew's cheek to bury itself in his thick black beard.

"Aah," said Joachim Gans, his hands dropping to his sides with finality. "We both have much to learn and much to explore. There are fools and those who only act like fools, to whatever purpose they may have hidden deep in their hearts. Which one am I? Which one are you? This is a mystery we must solve, and you will see there is no magic in it." He sighed again. "For what is the measure of a man? Have you become the sieve, boy, after all? Perhaps... if we search hard enough, together we might find the answers. Perhaps... there will be hope for us yet."

And the witches and demons, for once, were silent.

SONNET BY REIS COURTNEY

For what be measure of a man, you ask,
the lode of silver and of gold is nigh,
and deem it not a necessary task
to seek the shining metals where they lie?

Though oft times hidden in the darkest deep
the tangle of man's soul's a mystery.
There steps the bold explorer; might he weep
unraveling the skeins of history?

Thus stir the restless, fervent dreams of men
who search and seek, and none can e'er behold.
They stumble 'pon a serpent in its den
or else, a chalice of the purest gold.

Craftsmen ne'er perfected such an art
to sculpt the benchmark of a beating heart.

(As written by Reis Courtney, who ne'er considred himselfe a poete, by any manner thereof, in the yeare of Our Lord, 1601, 'pon fond remembrance of Joachim Gans, master metallurgist and mentore.)

EPILOGUE

AFTER SIR RICHARD Grenville sailed back to England in August, 1585, most likely taking some of the men with him, Ralph Lane and the remaining colonists set about gathering supplies for the approaching winter. But Ralph Lane lacked the diplomatic skills of negotiation. He angered the Indians to the point where Wingina, now known as Pemisapan, tried to gather support from the neighboring tribes in order to kill the explorers. However, he was not successful. Dependent for food and supplies on the alternating hostility and friendship of the natives, a desperate Lane and his men lasted through until the following spring.

Interestingly enough, by the time Sir Francis Drake's expedition landed at Roanoke in the spring, Lane and his followers had made a decision to stay. Becauseof this, Drake gave them a small ship which could negotiate the shallow channel; however, this ship disappeared in a hurricane.

Drake offered them another ship, larger than the first, which would have had to be anchored out in the Atlantic. Lane and his men became discouraged and, with the approach of yet another storm, quickly changed their minds and decided to leave with Drake. One week after they left so abruptly, a supply ship from England landed on Roanoke. The supply ship and Drake's fleet had crossed paths without sighting each other. Two weeks after that, Grenville's own fleet sailed up the Roanoke Sound to find a deserted camp.

The death of Pemisapan eased the threat to Lane's colony only on a temporary basis. Historians agree that most likely Lane's hostilities against the native tribes made it difficult for the 1587 Roanoke Island colony (known as the Lost Colony) to succeed, contributing to its ultimate failure. No trace of them was ever found. Both the 1585 Lane expedition and the 1587 Colony were declared unsuccessful.

The search for copper, which remained their focus, was in vain. The natives used copper for ornaments, for trade and for fashioning weapons and utensils. It appears that they were reluctant to tell where it could be found.

LETTERS PATENTS

Letters Patents,
Graunted by the Queenes Maiestie to Master Walter Ralegh
25 March 1584*

Elizabeth by the grace of God&c - To all people to whome these presentes shall come greting. Know yee that of our especiall grace certeyne science and mere mocyon We haue gyuen and graunted and by these presentes for vs our heyres and successors doe geve and grante to our trusty and welbeloved servaunte Walter Raleighe Esquier and to his heyres and ssignes for ever free liberty and license from tyme to tyme and at all tymes for ever hereafter to discover seach fynde out and viewe such remote heathen and barbarous landes Contries and territories not actually possessed of any Christian Prynce and inhabited by Christian people... Reseruing always to vs our heyres and successors for all seruives dueties and demaunles the fifte parte of all the owre of Gold and silver than from yme to tyme and at all tymes after such discovery subduying nd possessing shal be there gotten or obteyned... (In which

Elizabeth grants patents to Sir Walter Raleigh and asks for one fifth of all gold and silver he discovers)

*From: Quinn, David Beers, Ed.
The Roanoke Voyages 1584-1590. Vol. I

JOACHIM'S TALMUD*

The Talmud is a huge collection of doctrine and law, consisting of the teachings and opinions of thousands of rabbis on a great many varied subjects, including Halakha(law), ethics, philosophy, customs, history, lore and a number of other topics. The Talmud is the basis for all codes of Jewish law and is much quoted in rabbinic literature. These writings are as important to Jewish religious tradition as is the Bible's Old Testament, encompassing every subject explored in Jewish history.

Some of the basic areas covered are as follows:

    a. agricultural laws and rules for foods and blessings
    b. the rituals of the Sabbath and other holidays
    c. the issues between men and women, such as marriage and divorce
    d. issues of civil and criminal law
    e. laws of the temple
    f. laws of spiritual purity and impurity

Most orthodox Jews, such as Joachim Gans, found their wisdom in the Talmud. Joachim, no doubt, quoted freely from it. Being a deeply religious man, it is likely that he drew upon this intimate knowledge to govern his life and that of his young apprentice.

*"International Standard Bible Encyclopedia". 1915. Britannica.com: Encyclopedia article about "Talmud"

NORTH CAROLINA'S COASTAL INDIANS*

"In some respects the best-known Carolina Algonkian group, at least the one with which the Roanoke colonists had the most numerous contacts, was the so-called Secotan. This tribe's domain extended from Albemarle Sound to lower Pamlico River and from Roanoke Island to the west-central region of present Beaufort County.... The northeastern section of the peninsula between the Pamlico and Neuse Rivers was also a part of Secotan territory. Secotan distribution thus included the present counties of Washington, Tyrrell, Dare, and Hyde, the greater part of Beaufort, and the northern part of Pamlico.... The native inhabitants of the off-shore islands were geographically, and perhaps also culturally and politically, closer to the Secotan than to any other Algonkian group.

"Because of proximity to Roanoke the English colonists had closer contacts with the Secotan Indians than with any other tribe of the Carolina coast. Barlow's Wingandacoa is usually identified with Secotan, and most of the Indians whom he mentioned by name - Wingina, the chief, Granganimo, his brother, Wanchese and Manteo, the natives whom he took to England with him - were inhabitants of this area.... Hariot stated that most of his ethnological information pertained particularly to the coastal area in the vicinity of Roanoke, and

White's pictures of Indian scenes and subjects dealt largely with the towns of the Secotan tribe."

"ALGONKIAN ETHNOHISTORY OF THE CAROLINA SOUND" by Maurice A. Mook, Part 3 Journal of the Washington Academy of Sciences, Vol. 34, No. 6 (June 15, 1944), pp. 181-196, pp. 213-228.

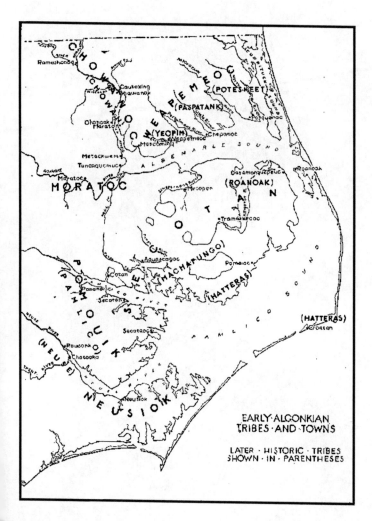

"Algonquian Ethnohistory of the Carolina Sound" by Maurice A. Mook, Journal of the Washington Academy of Sciences 34 (6–7), 1944.

PERSONNEL ASSOCIATED WITH THE 1585-86 VENTURE*

(Not all these people made the trip)
*names mentioned in the novel
*Sir Walter Ralegh
Sir Christopher Hatton
*Sir Francis Walsingham
Sir Philip Sidney, MP
Sir William Courtnay, MP
Sir William Mohun, MP
*John White, painter
*Sir Richard Grenville, general
*Simon Fernandez, chief pilot
John Clarke, Captain of Roebuck
Captain George Raymond, Captain of Lion of Chichester
Thomas Cavendish, Captain of Elizabeth
*Arthur Barlowe
Captain Boniten
Captain Aubry
John Arundell
John Stukely

Edward Gorges
*Master Bremige
Master Vincent
Captain John Copeltope
Edward, Scrivener
*Granganimeo
*Manteo
Richard Hakluyt, elder
Alonzo Cornieles, Captain of the Santa Maria of San
VicentEnrique Lopez, Portuguese merchant
Amyas Preston
Andrew Fulforde, Captain of Ralegh's Job
Kendall, gentleman
*Wingina
Master Francis Brooke, treasurer
John Stubbe
Peregrine Bertie, Lord Willoughby de Eresby
Martin Laurentson, Danish mbr of Grenville's expedition
Diego Menendez de Valdes

FURTHER READING

Donald, M. B.Elizabethan Copper: The History of The Company of Mines Royal, 1568-1605. London: Pergamon Press, Ltd. 1955.

Feuer, Lewis S. The Life and Works of Joachim Gaunse, Mining Technologist and First Recorded Jew in English-Speaking North America. Cincinnati: The American Jewish Archives, 1987.

Grassl, Gary."Joachim Gans of Prague: The first Jew in English America." American Jewish History: An American Jewish Historical Society Quarterly Publication. Johns Hopkins University Press, June 1998. Vol. 86, No. 2. pp. 195-217.

Hakluyt, Richard. Principall Navigations (1589), pp. 728-33 and (1600), III, p. 251, as quoted in Quinn, David, ed. The Roanoke Voyages 1584-1590, (The Hakluyt Society, London: 1955) Vo. I, pp. 115-116.

_____ Principall Navigations (1589) pp. 736-7, as quoted in Quinn, David, ed. The Roanoke Voyages 1584-1590, (The Hakluyt Society, London: 1955), Vol I, pp. 194-197.

Hoover, Herbert Clark. De Re Metallica, by Georgius Agricola. New York: & Lou, HenryDover Publications, 1950.

Humber, John L. Backgrounds and Preparations for the Roanoke Voyages, 1584-1590. Raleigh: North Caroline Dept. Of Cultural Resources, 1986.

Hume, Ivor Noel. "Roanoke Island: America's First Science Center." Colonial Williamsburg: Journal of the Colonial Williamsburg Foundation, Spring, 1994.

Jones, G. Lloyd. The Discovery of Hebrew in Tudor England: a third Language. Manchester: Manchester University Press, 1983.

Kertzer, Rabbi Morris N. What Is A Jew? A Guide to the Beliefs, Traditions and Practices of Judaism. New York: MacMillan Publishing Company, 1973.

Morrison, Samuel E. The European Discover of America: The Northern Voyages. New York: Oxford UniversityPress, 1971.

Mulholland, James A. A History of Metals in Colonial America. Alabama: The University of Alabama Press, 1981.

Quinn, David Beers. Set Faire for Roanoke. Chapel Hill: University of North Carolina, 1985.

_____ The Roanoke Voyages 1584-1590: Volumes I & II. New York: Dover Publications, 1991.

Roth, Cecil.The Jews in the Renaissance, New York: Harper & Row, 1959.

_____ A History of the Jews in England. Oxford: Clarendon Press, 1941.

Temple, John. Mining: An international History. London, 1972.

White, John. "John White's Narrative of the 1587 Virginia Voyage (1587)," as quoted in

Wolf, Lucien. "Jews in Elizabethan England," Presidential Address, Nov. 21, 1926, in The Jewish Historical Society of England Transactions, Sessions 1924-27, Vol. XI, 1928. London: Spottiswoode, Ballantyne & Co.

The Universal Jewish Encyclopedia. New York: The Universal Jewish Encyclopedia, Inc., 1941.

ABOUT THE AUTHOR AND ILLUSTRATOR

M. L. Stainer is the well-known author of *The Lyon Saga*, a series of five books about The Lost Colony of Roanoke Island, North Carolina, circa 1587. *The LyonSaga* has been endorsed by the North Carolina Department of Public Instruction and has received highly acclaimed reviews, including School Library Journal. Joachim's Magic is her newest novel for young adults and deals with the earlier Ralph Lane expedition of 1585. It concerns Queen Elizabeth I's metallurgist, Joachim Gans, who was the first recorded Jew in the New World.

"When I write, I escape into a world all my own. It's a great joy," says the author. Ms. Stainer lives in the lower Hudson Valley area of beautiful New York State with her husband, Frank, and a menagerie of beloved dogs and cats. Born in London, she holds numerous degrees from Queens College, New Paltz and Fordham University. She's a retired high school English teacher with many young adult novels to her credit. She writes under the pseudonym M. L. Stainer to honor her father.

www.chickensouppress.net

James Melvin, who did the cover design and illustrations for the book, lives in Nags Head, North Carolina, where he operates Melvin's Studio and Gallery. He always dreamed of becoming an artist. He received his formal training from North Carolina's A & T State University in 1970. For several years this degree was put to use while James served as a Peace Corps art instructor in Botswana, Africa.

He is well-known for his stunning portrayals of black culture and life. A versatile artist, he works in oils, acrylics and pastels, and has illustrated many children's books. He was commissioned by the North Carolina Department of Cultural Resources to paint *Raleigh's Venture,* a celebration of 400 years since the founding of the Roanoke Colony. Melvin's works are owned by collectors throughout the U.S. and abroad.

www.melvinsstudio.com

READ MORE ABOUT JOACHIM GANS IN
JOACHIM: THE HERETIC

When Joachim returns to England, he seeks an audience with Elizabeth I. Taking Reis Courtney with him as his apprentice, he finds himself in Bristol working on new ways to make saltpeter. Trouble begins when, at a local inn, he refuses to affirm Christ as the Son of God. He is tried first in Bristol but, not knowing what to do with him, the officials send him to London to be judged a blasphemer by the members of the Queen's Privy Council. No conclusion is reached and the Council releases him. In the aftermath, Joachim decides to return to his native Bohemia. Reis, in the meantime, finds work as a horse trainer for one gentleman farmer, Robert Marchette, building a new life and future for himself.

CPSIA information can be obtained
at www.ICGtesting.com
Printed in the USA
FFOW02n1553280216
21929FF